Michael Stephens is presently living in Sydney with his family. He is a full-time writer, looks after his two sons, and occasionally takes on speaking engagements.

BLAT
MAGIC

MICHAEL STEPHENS

Angus&Robertson
An imprint of HarperCollins*Publishers,* Australia

First published in Australia in 2001
by HarperCollins*Publishers* Pty Limited
ABN 36 009 913 517
A member of the HarperCollins*Publishers* (Australia) Pty Limited Group
http://www.harpercollins.com.au

HarperCollins*Publishers*
25 Ryde Road, Pymble, Sydney, NSW 2073, Australia
31 View Road, Glenfield, Auckland 10, New Zealand
77–85 Fulham Palace Road, London W6 8JB, United Kingdom
Hazelton Lanes, 55 Avenue Road, Suite 2900, Toronto, Ontario M5R 3L2
and 1995 Markham Road, Scarborough, Ontario M1B 5M8, Canada
10 East 53rd Street, New York NY 10022, USA

National Library of Australia Cataloguing-in-Publication data:

Stephens, Michael.
    Blat magic.
    ISBN 0 207 19725 3.
    I. Title.
A823.3

Cover illustration by Nigel Buchanan
Typeset by HarperCollins*Publishers* in 12.5/14.5pt Matrix
Printed and bound in Australia by Griffin Press on 79gsm Bulky Paperback White

4 3 2 1
04 03 02 01

To Lila, with love

PART ONE

ONE ~~~

As she ran into the heart of Deep Forest, the woman pressed a bundle to her chest with one hand and grasped a thin-bladed sword with the other. The wind howled through branches, sometimes angry, sometimes sad. It was midnight.

Even if there had been enough light, she could not have seen over the tree roots that covered the forest floor. With each trunk big enough to contain a mansion of rooms and staircases, balconies and hallways, furniture and carpets, the woman was tiny by comparison.

Storm clouds grumbled as the wind strained to herd them across the sky. Occasionally a gap allowed moonlight to touch the forest floor.

The woman kissed the bundle, murmured a few words instantly snatched away by the thunder, and set off again.

High above, an owl bumped his head against a branch, nearly dropped the hessian sack that he was carrying over his back, and whimpered: 'This weather! This night! Please end. *End.*' With a hoot of determination, he straightened the sack and set off again. Tangles of branches and tree trunks made travel lower down in the forest impossible for an overburdened owl.

He halted on a branch and froze, listening.

'Wolves. So now it's wolves,' he muttered. His beak remained half open in horror.

Growling blended with thunder to make it seem as if the whole world had grown teeth. Yellow eyes glared up. Once again the owl nearly dropped the sack.

But instead he grasped it more firmly and set off, like the woman, ever deeper into the forest.

TWO ~~~

A wolf howled, summoning other packs from their comfortable dens. Eyes glinted with each lightning bolt, and black lips snarled back from teeth. They had scented an intruder! Well, they would soon do something about that.

When the woman heard the wolves, she tightened her grip on the sword and slowed, taking care not to stumble. Now and then she halted to whisper soothing words, and once even to hum a tune, face close to the bundle.

Then she saw the eyes of a wolf, barely two trees away. She jumped to a tree root, and gazed searchingly around.

Then she stood still.

Before the wolf could know where exactly she was, she had slung the bundle to her back, pushed the sword into its sheath, and was climbing, clinging to cracks in the bark. When she reached a hollow in a tree trunk, nearly three yards from the ground, she laid the bundle down, and stroked it. Then she unsheathed the sword and pushed the sword-tip into a knot in the blanket. Standing on her toes, she carefully raised the bundle to a wide fork just above. That high, it might just be safe from wolves.

Up here the bark became too smooth for her to climb. Gently, she patted the bundle with the sword-tip.

'Farewell, my darling,' she called out, and in a second she was off, among the tree roots, running faster now that she no longer had to worry about keeping whatever she had been carrying safe.

Two trees away, she called out:

'Wolves! Wolves! Why are you so stupid? Don't you have noses? *Here I am!*' And she raced over roots and rocks which, to someone of her size, were ramparts and hills.

The wolves' legs were much longer than those of the woman. In fact, she was barely half as tall as a newborn wolf cub.

Clutching the sack in both claws, the owl glided lower. Lightning showed him the backs of hurrying wolves.

'She's leading them away,' he muttered, half in horror and half in awe. He rested the sack on a branch and stood still. About to fly off, leaving the sack behind, the roaring and barking of the wolves became so loud suddenly that he pressed his wings to his ears to avoid hearing.

When the noise had stopped he gave a mournful hoot.

THREE ~~~

Cliffmabakin de Mandiargues, Cliffkin for short, was asleep in a smallish bedroom a third of the way up Number 14, Drimsen Pallisades. Beside his bed was half a cup of cold tea, pale-milky on its surface, and a plate holding crumbs from a piece of strawberry shortcake. The window was open a hand's-breadth, and the shutters were pinned back. Unlike most of the blats who for centuries had made their homes in Deep Forest, Cliffkin relished storms. If a puddle of rain water gathered on his windowsill, and even if it overflowed to his floor, that was a small price to pay for the luxury of what he called 'cosying up', which meant lying warm and safe in bed while listening to the blast of a storm's music. Because of this habit, Cliffkin was the only blat in the whole of Deep Forest to hear the wolves.

As he sat up, he used his fingers to comb away the reddish hair, streaked with grey, that fell over his eyes and either side of his long, blat nose.

'*Wolves* ...?' he wondered. Wolves only made noises like that when they were hunting, or fighting one another, and what rabbit or vole, what creature of any sort, let alone an invading army of wolves, would be out in a storm like this? He pushed the window further open. As a flurry of rain caught him in the face he made out part of a cry:

'Wolves!'

Someone was down there. It sounded like a woman, calling out.

Not really knowing what he was about to do, Cliffkin grabbed a pair of trousers, tugged them over his nightshirt, and rushed to the door.

A gust of stormy wind pushed him back, flew around the room, and knocked something over. He hesitated on the verandah, grasping the railing. Like an assembly of warning fingers, branches and twigs shook madly.

What can you hope to do? An old man like you? Go back to bed! Pretend you didn't hear a thing!

Instead he took a deep breath, raised his arms above his head, and dived.

He glided through darkness, caught hold of one branch and swung to another. Walking, he had seemed unsure of himself, even weak; now, despite his age, he moved as gracefully as an acrobat.

He knew every branch, every twig, for miles around. This was where he had grown up and first learned to

6

swing through trees. It was his special territory; his and his ancestors' own part of Deep Forest.

Soon he was low enough to see (as a bolt of lightning crackled) the gleam of wolves' teeth. Then eyes flashed at him and, snarling, the pack coiled like a dreadful living engine over the ground.

'Where are you?' Cliffkin shouted. 'Where are you?'

No reply.

He travelled slowly, following the wolves. Lightning flashed now and then, or moonlight shone from a tear in the clouds, briefly showing him a wolf racing between rocks or around a tree. He heard growling, but nothing more of the woman until, from nearby, but far down, came a wail, followed by enraged barking.

Cliffkin jumped down from branch to branch until he was in the Nantle's tree, beside a 'For Sale' sign. He heard the wailing again, and for the first time tonight, indeed for the first time in many years, he was terrified.

Wolves could not climb trees, but they could get a surprisingly long way up them with a running start. (It was one of the first lessons taught every young blat: Never rely on a wolf's inability to climb. The next was: Never think that a wolf is stupid.)

Cliffkin stared into darkness.

It was years since he had been this close to the ground.

Then he heard it again, directly below. Must be just above the roots, he told himself with a gloomy laugh.

Out of the question to go that far down.

Nevertheless he found himself descending, pushing like the expert climber he was at each bark foothold before entrusting his weight to it, descending towards a wailing that with its frail helplessness, the way it quivered and hiccuped, belonged — even to Cliffkin's ears, inexperienced on this subject as they were — to a baby.

The wolves would reach it at any moment.

'Reach me too,' he told himself.

So why weren't they here? Had the woman deliberately — and this was the first time he thought it, though it later became a conviction — enticed the wolves away rather than risk a dangerous and slow climb, with the baby, into the safety of the trees?

The crying was coming from a fork in the tree trunk. As he pushed at a ridge of bark to see if it would take his weight, a pack of hunter-wolves arrived below and halted, sniffing the smell-laden air.

A blat, their noses told them, not far above, certainly reachable. Below the blat was something that did not smell blattish, was smaller, yet promised to be edible all the same. They planted their front paws wide apart for extra jumping strength. They only hesitated because, for the moment, they couldn't believe their luck.

Cliffkin knew there was nothing he could do.

Full of regret for the work he would leave behind (he thought, in particular, of his two rows of desk drawers) he stared back at the wolves and surprised himself by shouting:

'So go on! Attack! What are you afraid of?'

The animals had begun to spring when something flew past Cliffkin from above, and he heard the words, as distinct as anything:

'Close your eyes!'

So he did. And a second later the world (as seen

through the blat's eyelids) became entirely red, and a deep 'Boom!' rumbled from below, followed by what felt like handfuls of dirt thrown into his face.

'There we are,' came a voice, as papery stuff lightly brushed his cheek.

Opening one eye, he saw nothing, the dazzle against his eyelids had been so great. Then he made out a curved beak and a flash of white from great, round eyes. An owl was beside him, a pocket-owl exactly his height. On the ground, lumps of red, like coals from an old fire, were still glowing.

Now the wailing started up again.

'Aren't you going to fetch it?' demanded the owl. 'In a minute or two the wolves will be able to see again.' Using his beak and one claw, balancing on a single leg with the help of his wings, he was drawing a string tight around the top of a bulging hessian sack, sealing it up. 'There'll be new wolves, too,' he muttered, 'and I don't want to have to stand here all night throwing potatoes.'

Cliffkin climbed down as the temporarily blinded animals, snarling and blinking, bumped into one another, and in the tree-fork he found a bundle of blankets not much longer than his forearm.

At one end was the face of a baby, all except forehead and nose in shadow.

No time to wonder. He tucked the baby into the crook of his arm and climbed back up the tree to where the owl had just succeeded in knotting the top of his bag.

'Be quiet, please,' the bird snapped.

The baby squirmed, struggling to get its hands free of the tightly wrapped-around blanket.

Certainly was strong, for a baby, Cliffkin decided.

The storm whipped and shoved upper branches, and sent down heavy drops of rain.

After listening for long seconds, the owl let his head fall onto his chest. Just as Cliffkin was about to start asking questions, the owl said:

'You know, I don't think she wanted to live.' And he turned his scholarly eyes on Cliffkin. 'She'd heard about you. You're Cliffkin, aren't you? She was strong, and too brave for her own good. But she was disillusioned. I called to her, but she wouldn't answer. I can't tell you any more. Who was she? That must be a secret for a long, long time. You will see me again. I'll find a place to live, nearby. Don't tell anyone about this. You found a child, that's all. I suppose you know how to look after a baby? Anyway, you can learn.'

'What?' Cliffkin wondered. 'What do you mean, look after —?'

But the owl had flapped off into the dark, clutching the hessian sack in both claws.

FOUR ~~~

Cliffkin sat down on his bed and folded the blanket away from the baby's face.

Smaller than even the tiniest blat-baby's, the nose wasn't in the least pointed like a blat's. It resembled a human's, in fact, but this baby was far too small to be human.

Most likely it was a merryn, one of that race of short, human-like creatures who live in big cities and specialise, because of their tiny fingers, in watch repairs and microelectronics.

The baby looked back at Cliffkin with emerald green eyes. Its hair was long, black, and wispy thin. Cliffkin sighed.

'What am I to do with you?'

'Da,' replied the baby.

Cliffkin almost smiled, until he remembered the woman who had led the wolves away and had almost certainly died in doing so. According to the owl she had come here on purpose.

'She'd heard of you,' the owl had said.

'Da,' went the baby, then, 'Dada!'

Cliffkin shook his head. 'No, I can't possibly look after you. I'm a sorcerer, mostly retired. I've lived alone for many years — since my parents died. I have no experience of babies.'

Cliffkin lowered his voice. 'I'll ring Madam. That's what I'll do.'

He picked up the steam-powered telephone beside his bed and dialled a number.

'Madam? It's me. Something ... strange has happened. Can you come, right away?'

Very soon, there was a knocking at the door.

'What a storm!' Madam Mambrol lifted a damp shawl from her head and shoulders, then picked a sopping fragment of bark from the back of one hand as she asked:

'What's that?'

She was a head shorter than Cliffkin, and quite a bit wider. Waistcoat of dark gold, a red shirt, and her skirt was the green of topmost leaves when the sun is setting.

'It's a baby, Madam.'

'Well, you'd better tell me about it. But first, I need to wash my hands, and to drink a strong cup of tea.'

She went to the kitchen, followed by Cliffkin.

'Don't tell me yet.' As the kettle started to boil, she marched over and gazed again at the bundle.

'Not a blat. Not a merryn either.'

As she poured the tea, her eyes seemed as vague as the steam that curled from the cups, but an instant later they were sharp with concentration. She was two years older than the sorcerer and, although not related, had since their schooldays been both friend and older sister to him. They had met above the Year Two platform, Cliffkin searching for a golf ball that he had hit in a ridiculous direction. She had given him one of her own so that he wouldn't get into trouble. Now she was a doctor at the East Fork Hospital, but her free time was spent in collecting, writing down and telling the legends that many older blats knew by heart but which, with the coming of TV (two hundred and sixty-five years ago) they had begun to forget.

Like most blats, Madam was an expert golfer. Five years ago she had won the Open Twilight Championship, one of the most difficult of all golfing contests due to the ball being nearly invisible in the dusk.

Once they had moved back into Cliffkin's bed-sitting room she held out her arms. 'I'd better have a look. Get me a towel please.'

The still fast asleep baby was wearing a white nightdress. Madam fingered the material.

'Silk, from Nalmian worms fed on crickleberry leaves, I'd say. Worth a fortune. Nappy needs changing.' She ran her fingers back and forth along the edge of the towel, then ripped it cleanly in half. 'While I change the nappy, tell me where you found him.'

As Cliffkin spoke, the baby blinked at Madam, then dozed off. When she had changed his nappy, using half the towel, Madam handed him back to Cliffkin and folded the other half up for a spare.

'You'd better get used to holding him,' she advised. 'Babies need a great deal of holding.'

Cliffkin peered at the tiny, sleeping creature, and suddenly wanted someone to hold *him*.

'But I don't know anything —'

'Commonsense takes care of most of it, my old friend. To look after a baby, you need to be devoted, that's the main thing. You can't mind being woken during the night, nor a million interruptions throughout the day. That only lasts for about a year, until they can crawl around, then you have to stop them falling off branches. On the way, you must teach them one or two little things, such as a whole language, how to hold a fork, and which things are good to eat, which poisonous. Then they go to school and there are new worries. But that's years away. You don't have to think about that yet.' She gave the baby a thoughtful look. 'This one's about, I'd say, a month old. Perhaps younger, although not quite a newborn. So why not make his birthday a month ago?

'And we can't keep on calling him "him",' she resumed, giving the bundle an especially thoughtful look. 'We'd better think of a name. Family name, de Mandiargues, of course, but first and middle? I'll get us some more tea — or coffee this time, to make us extra alert — while you think up a first and a middle name.'

'But . . .'

As he stared again at the bundle, Cliffkin had a sudden sense of how the world must look from high above the treetops of Deep Forest. (He was a dreamy sort of blat who, especially during a crisis, was prone to visions of this sort.)

The world looked cold and vast. Most of it was dark green, but there were oceans too, so deep that no-one knew how deep they were. Eagles, falcons and hawks circled forests and grassy plains in quest of prey. Wolves and, in some places, snakes, controlled the forest floor. Mountains reached for, then soared above, the highest possible layer of cloud. Some were made entirely of dark blue ice, and were so cold that no animal could possibly survive on them. In vast cities full of humans and other animals, the streets were lit by electric lamps and patrolled by machines with powerful lights that, to an ignorant blat, resembled eyes. Compared to this enormous world, a baby, especially a blat-sized one, was little more than a speck. Without someone to take care of it, how could it live? And if he, Cliffkin, didn't look after it, who would?

'You wouldn't ...?' he began tentatively, when Madam returned with the coffee.

'Be careful to keep hot liquids away from him,' she continued. 'Babies reach out suddenly, and grab. Wouldn't what? Look after it? Love to, of course. But I haven't been chosen — you have. I'll help you, any way I can, but you're the parent. That's what the owl said, isn't it? You're the one who takes responsibility, which means that you get the blame, and the sadness, if something goes wrong. Have you thought of a name?'

An hour ago Cliffkin had been a sorcerer who liked reading history books, watching golf on TV (although he wasn't much good at playing it), and who lived contentedly by himself.

Suddenly he was a father, thinking up a name for a baby.

'Something simple,' Madam continued, 'that won't get him teased in the playground. What about "Kolsimographlex"?'

'So *am* I going to look after it?' Cliffkin wondered to himself. 'A son, am I going to have a *son*?'

'Cliffkin?'

'Yes?'

'Kolsimographlex? As a first name, I mean. Then he could be called Kolsi for short.' Madam blew on her coffee.

'Kolsimographlex...' Cliffkin repeated, pretending to give the name serious thought.

Hands unwrapping a parcel ...

Cliffkin suddenly remembered his own mother in the doorway of their old house, Number 32 Byway Grove, sunlight falling onto her strong hands as she unfolded and tore at dark blue paper. Aged three or four, Cliffkin had asked, 'What is it? A present? Can I have it?'

Inside was a little bell made of gold on a gold chain. Coiled around the clapper was wire to prevent it from ringing. 'You only have to pull out the wire,' his mother had explained, 'to make it ring. It's *extremely* precious, and, yes, one day it will be yours. But you must only ring it when you're in the most terrible danger. You'll remember that, won't you?'

'What is it? Where does it come from?'

'Pinguel,' she answered. 'It's a word in Old Blat, meaning "gift". I got it in return for a favour that I did someone, a long time ago.'

He had been about to ask, 'What language? What favour?', when his fascination with the bell took over.

15

His mother had found a glass case for it, with a lockable door. Now the precious bell, which his mother had called 'The Ant Bell' without ever explaining why, stood on Cliffkin's mantelpiece.

This remembering took hardly long enough for Madam to give an affectionate sigh, and to wonder how long her friend would be absent, this time, in his daydreaminess.

'Pinguel,' said Cliffkin.

'As a name?' Madam looked at the ceiling. 'Mmmm. Doesn't it mean something?'

'"Gift" in Old Blat.' He looked down, and was shocked to discover that the baby looked blurry. Yes, there were tears in his own, grown-up eyes.

Madam put a hand on her friend's shoulder.

'A good name. Pinguel, Pinguel de Mandiargues. Won't be teased at school. In fact, a beautiful name.'

At the centre of the topmost shelf above Cliffkin's desk, surrounded by valuable chunks of amber containing insects so ancient that their species no longer existed, the Ant Bell stood in its glass case. As Cliffkin and Madam discussed Pinguel, the bell glinted in a deeply golden way that (to an expert in such bells) meant only one thing.

The time was coming when, across forests and oceans and stormy skies, the wire would have to be removed and the bell rung.

PART TWO

FIVE ~~~

Blats do not like to worry about the future. They can plan, and hoard, but when it comes to wringing their hands and feeling anxious, they don't enjoy it, and aren't especially good at it. They prefer to concentrate on what is right in front of them, and if anything unpleasant does happen, they have confidence in their 'melting abilities', that famous blat capacity to blend into their surroundings so that they are almost undetectable not only by other creatures, but also by misfortune in general.

But Madam Mambrol was different. She thought about the world's dangers, and even spoke of them.

'Sometimes I think —' she began one day when they were all at her place and Pinguel was eight months old.

She interrupted herself to point to the baby, who had crawled beneath the TV set and, with the stub of a lead pencil, was trying to dig his way into the underside.

'Pinguel! Stop!' Cliffkin called out.

The eyes of the human newsreader flickered as though the man was scared of what this baby might do to him.

'Doe! Doe!' Pinguel cried.

As Cliffkin lifted him away from the screen, the baby twisted around and hurled his pencil, catching the human between the eyes.

Madam held out her saucer. 'Here, Pinguel, have some cake.'

Now the screen showed a pyramid bristled around with traffic lights, roundabouts and road signs. A voice proclaimed:

'Witness the latest monument erected in honour of Lord Pinchie du Henderson!'

A close-up showed a colourful portrait of what looked like a giant human clothed in a long cloak made up of brilliant streaks of yellow, red and lime green. His face was old, with hollow cheeks and a curved-over, thin nose.

'Sometimes I feel,' Madam continued, 'that we blats are surrounded in this forest, with no hope of escape. I know,' she admitted, 'it's only a mood. It'll pass. But ever since Pinguel, and especially if I wake up early, and can't get back to sleep, I feel that we're in danger.'

Cliffkin wondered if Madam was consulting him as a sorcerer; whether, for instance, she wanted a potion that would give her happier dreams.

'I suppose it comes from reading the Annals,' she went on. 'In our history, a long period of peace and prosperity is usually followed by turmoil and trouble, isn't it? Though perhaps now is diff—'

Before Madam could say, '—erent', a broad, cheerful face appeared at a window:

'Sister!'

'Strolgo. Just in time.' Madam let in her brother, a tall, broad-shouldered blat who had a tin helmet fastened to his belt and was carrying on his shoulders a baby of about Pinguel's age, though quite a bit bigger.

'Estana's taken the little ones to golf.' Strolgo's face was long, with a squarish chin that told you immediately how stubborn he could be. He was a captain in the Spear Guard, in charge of a unit of twenty-five professional soldiers. *Just in time for what?* he wondered, struggling with the baby in his arms who was reaching out for his regular playmate.

He placed him on the floor, and Cliffkin did the same with Pinguel. As the adults watched, the babies stared at one another, lowered their heads, and began to crawl. But while Ogren went towards Pinguel, Pinguel crawled backwards, away from his friend.

'Ah, still hasn't learned how to go forwards?' Strolgo accepted a slice of cake. As he sat down, the springs in the armchair creaked beneath his weight.

'Now, what am I just in time for? Apart from afternoon tea.'

Madam pointed to the TV. 'It's those pyramids and Lord Grand the Supreme Duke Pinchie du Henderson, or whatever he's called. One day he'll want to conquer Deep Forest, won't he? Such things do happen, you know — if you read the Annals — from time to time.'

Strolgo blinked at the screen, and politely, though without much success, tried to look worried.

'That reminds me. Know who I met the other day? Old Sarin, the last of the Far Scouts. Remember him setting off on his journeys when we were children? We chatted over a mint julep, and there was one of those things in the corner' — Strolgo pointed at the TV — 'and do you know what Sarin told me? "Pay no attention, my dear Strolgo," he said. "None of it's true — the human stuff — and I mean *none*." In his days as a Far Scout, he told me, he'd seen beyond the forest, and it was utterly different. "Smokestacks and slave labour," he told me. "Blackness and grime. Heaps of poisonous metal glowing in the dark. knights on black horses wielding spiky things on the end of chains."

'Ah —' Strolgo held out both hands, palms out, to fend off objections. 'I know what people say: that Sarin went

21

mad, that he couldn't take the loneliness of being a Far Scout. Well, I don't agree. I think there is a good deal of sense in that old head. Anyway, I know one of his strange stories that is true beyond any doubt.'

Strolgo spread his fingers over his helmet, waiting for someone to ask him to go on.

To everyone's surprise, it was Pinguel, kneeling, who provided the encouragement:

'Doe?'

Strolgo ruffled the baby's long, black hair. 'Now *that's* what I call brainy!'

After touching Pinguel, the warrior moved his hand away just a fraction faster than he would have if it had been a blat baby. Blats weren't used to dealing with non-blats; Pinguel would take some getting used to. Cliffkin often wondered what exactly this would mean for the boy as he grew up.

'Yes,' Strolgo went on, 'Sarin told me that an *owl* has taken up residence not far from the fifty-second hole of the Old Course, half a mile from Dragon's Tooth, on the south side. I told the others in my squad, but none believed me, so I went there, and what do you think I found? Yes, an *owl*, living hardly any distance from the leaf tips.'

When Strolgo left, Pinguel stretched out his arms as usual towards his playmate, Ogren, imploring him not to go.

Madam could guess what Cliffkin was about to say.

'Yes, yes, I'll mind the baby. You go and see the owl.' She laid a hand on her friend's arm and spoke with emotion the usual blat words for a short farewell:

'Watch the branches!' But she added: '*Most carefully.*'

'I will,' answered the sorcerer as he stepped from the doorstep into empty space, and fell.

In the time of Cliffkin's grandparents the trees around Dragon's Tooth had been full of blats. Now the remains of their platforms, furnaces, steam-pipes, golf courses and cable car stops sagged, ragged with age and overgrown with moss and fungi. Eagles, falcons, and especially the hawks who nest along the razor sharp crevasses of the tooth-like spur (nowadays feeding mostly on young crab beetles whose shells were still soft enough for them to be eaten whole) had eventually forced the blats to move. According to blat history that children learned at school, what was called 'The Bird Menace' had finished with a great blat victory, known as 'The Victory of Camster's Knee', in which the birds had been forced to give up their control of parts of the forest in return for blat promises not to disturb them in their nests around the spur.

The victory took its strange name from a corporal in a blat warrior squad, Camster, who when captured by a hawk and lifted high above the trees had kept his nerve, continuing to fight 'with typical blat ferocity', so that the hawk, defeated more by the blat's courage and refusal to be frightened, had dropped him back into the trees. The hawk had grabbed Camster by his knee, which had afterwards remained a little stiff, causing the blat to walk with a limp. Camster's bravery had been typical of the spirit shown by blat warriors, and the hawks had been forced to make a treaty.

That was what the history books said, but Cliffkin had lived for long enough among his fellow blats, and was wise enough, to suspect that it wasn't the whole truth. Blats had certainly given up the forest around Dragon's Tooth. Perhaps something had happened to the knee of a blat called Camster. But in Cliffkin's experience blats were not ferocious. In fact, they avoided even the threat of, let alone actual violence.

The Tooth was a narrow ridge of rock that jutted for miles into the forest. As he neared it, Cliffkin was careful to keep below the treetops. Up there, leaves shone green-gold, and patches of evening sky gleamed, blue turning to mauve.

Abandoned houses and platforms cast ghostly, sad shadows. A door hung off its hinges, and, inside, fungus had sprouted from floorboards. Broken windows gaped onto vacant interiors. The few shards of glass that remained were so dirty they looked like stone.

Cliffkin glimpsed a window that glowed with light. The forest was silent. A door stood open onto a platform with built-up sides and containing black earth and what he recognised as potato plants.

Absorbing the lonely mood of the place, Cliffkin made himself nearly invisible. The light inside the tree was deep yellow. He crept closer.

Seated in an armchair that had been patched up with so many different materials that it was impossible to see what colour it had originally been, an owl was holding a fat book in his wings. Behind him stood a bookcase; on the desk was an ink pot, an old-fashioned quill pen, and a sheet of paper. The owl turned a page and, without looking up, spoke:

'Owls have the sharpest eyes in the world. Good afternoon. I've been expecting you.' He held out a wing.

'Come in. We didn't have much time for introductions the last time we met. My name is Sogforstinful de los Ambriames, but please call me Sog. And you are Cliffkin, the sorcerer. Sit down, while I get us some tea.

'I'm a scholar,' he called from the kitchen, 'so I'm used to being alone. You know, I might have become too used to it for my own good.' He returned, carrying a tray. 'I come from faraway, where there are no blats, but I've heard of you. There are blats the other side of the Cold Mountains, did you know?'

'No,' Cliffkin answered, astonished, as he took a cup of tea.

'I've seen them,' the owl continued, 'and studied their Annals, what's more. In their forest, snakes — vipers especially — rule the ground. Their trees are more ancient than yours. The Outside World is closer to them — only by a little way, but still closer. It's creeping up on you, too.

'Hmm.' With the handle of a teaspoon, the owl stroked the white feathers on his chin. 'But you came to ask about Pinguel, I suppose, not to listen to a rambling old bird.'

'What you say is fascinating, but ... Please.' Suddenly Cliffkin felt frightened, and wondered if he wanted to know the answer to the question he was about to ask:

'Who *is* Pinguel? *What* is he? He isn't a blat, I know. Where did he come from?'

Cliffkin's light green, blat's eyes warned the owl: Remember that whatever you are about to tell me, Pinguel is now *mine*. I have become more than just a babysitter. I am too fond of him to give him up.

This emotion was also expressed in a slight trembling

at the tip of his long, blat's nose, something that only happened when he was angry or frightened.

Over the past eight months little things had piled up around Cliffkin to make a new life. When he thought of home, he now thought not just of his apartment, but of Pinguel too.

As Sog observed these emotions in the old blat, he nodded with approval, and extended a surprisingly long wing to pat Cliffkin's shoulder.

'No cause for worry. You were chosen. By the way' — with a thoughtful air, he touched the paper on his desk — 'I like the name. Pinguel. Old Blat, isn't it? Well, to answer your question, Who is he? Why, your son.' The owl widened his eyes. 'Has no other father, none at all, and no mother either. You are his father, and whenever he hears that word, for the rest of his life, he will think of you.'

The owl gave a little shake of his head. He had become entangled in the emotion of what he was saying. He freed himself with a shrug and went on:

'He'll be blat-sized, but that's about all he'll have in common with blats, I think. Where does he come from? Well, that's a secret. For the safety of blats, I don't want to say. Let this be enough: the place no longer exists. It has been destroyed. Once it was magnificent, and powerful, and believed to be entirely safe from the Outside World. Now it is gone.

'Where was I? Yes, *what* is he, your Pinguel? Another secret: all I can tell you is that he's a fugitive, like those other fugitives whom you, and other blat sorcerers in the past, have from time to time helped. Oh yes, I know all about that. So did Pinguel's mother, and that's why she came here. But I'd better not say any more. One day, I promise, it will be clear. Now let's drink our tea and talk about the weather, like good forest-dwellers.'

SIX ~~~

While Cliffkin had tea with Sog, the telephone whistled back at Madam Mambrol's. She made sure that Pinguel was all right (he had once again crawled himself backwards under the sofa) and went into the next room to answer it.

When she had gone, baby Pinguel, hardly eight months old, examined a dust ball. When he breathed out, it tumbled away. If he sucked in his breath he could make it come closer.

Then he noticed his legs. Until now, knees had been the most important. After all, they are what push you around the floor.

Now he glimpsed his toes.

He wriggled them. They were under his control. He owned them.

Then he remembered Cliffkin leaving the room. The sorcerer's toes had been hidden beneath shoes with curling-over tips that Pinguel quite enjoyed chewing when they were still. But from seeing Cliffkin getting dressed in the morning, and undressed at night, Pinguel knew that toes lay underneath.

Thoughtfully, Pinguel crawled (backwards). Something important was about to happen, he could feel it.

He held onto an arm of the sofa and pulled. At the same time he brought his legs underneath and pushed down with his new-found toes.

He was travelling upwards. And he could already see much that until now had been concealed from him. On the sofa were white squares with straggly black lines across them (old blat fables, written out by Madam).

Cliffkin had left the room. It saddened Pinguel whenever he saw his father depart. He knew that he would see him again soon, but it saddened him all the same.

He let go of the sofa and took the first step of his life.

He staggered — this was itself a surprise, not to be going backwards — then halted and, miraculously, did not fall. He felt himself swaying, as if there were giant hands rocking the floor. Without actually saying the words to himself, he realised that either he had to keep moving or tumble over. So he continued towards the door through which Strolgo, then his friend Ogren, and finally Cliffkin, had departed.

He hardly had time to notice that it was getting dark, and that a tree branch, flattened at its top, curled into the shadows, and that directly ahead was a low railing. He felt the bristly WELCOME mat beneath his feet, but had no time to work out what it was before he felt himself falling, falling.

He hit his shoulder painfully against a branch, then caught his arm along something hard yet also slippery with a sort of black stuff. He found himself looking into a well-lit, yellow room full of empty seats. He knew what this was. A cable car, an empty one. He was lying on a roof-window.

The automatic cable car halted at a high platform made of woven twigs, and turned out its light. Pinguel went to crawl onto a branch, half expecting to go backwards instead. He gave a cry of delight, startling a pair of blue finches on a nearby twig, when he found himself going forwards. He reached the platform, and pulled himself up. He was high, higher than he'd ever been. Across a branch lay deep red light from the setting sun. He tottered towards this, fascinated.

From far below came a sound that was familiar, but he was too entranced by the red light to pay attention. It was Madam, shouting his name.

Soon the branches thinned out, until only twigs remained. Above him was a vast roof, red on one side and black on the other as though a silent battle between these two colours was taking place. Black was winning: overhead was wholly dark.

As Pinguel watched, the red began to fade. He was about to turn away, disappointed, when he noticed a milky light on a leaf beside his face. Where did it come from? Raising his head, he was shocked to see (encased in the blackness that a moment ago had looked so complete) a single point of silver. He raised his hand. The back of it caught the light. He turned, and had to clutch onto twigs not to fall back from amazement.

A gigantic silvery-white face, round as a saucer, was staring down at him. Eyes and mouth were faded grey, as though the head was many, many miles distant. No body, only a head, floating.

'Doe?' Pinguel called out to it.

It didn't reply.

Air stroked his cheeks, then something more solid, but still soft. Then hard, pointed instruments grasped his arm so tightly that it hurt, and pulled him up above the twigs.

29

'Ow!' he called out. Reaching up, he grabbed a handful of soft stuff, and at the same time saw what was carrying him.

It was Peter Hawk, from the legends that Madam Mambrol read out. Pinguel had not yet worked out what Peter was supposed to have done that made him so famous, but he did remember his picture. Here was the same curved-over beak, clever, round eyes, and feathers shaped like the tips of Strolgo's arrows.

Cold air howled in Pinguel's ears; he was travelling fast. He pulled at the bird's feathers with his free hand, laughed, heard a loud squawk, and suddenly felt himself among leaves and twigs, then lying stomach-down across a branch.

A wind fluttered over him, and, quite far away, against the silver face in the sky, was the profile of Peter Hawk peering down.

Pinguel couldn't understand what caused him to remain silent and still. He sensed that it was the best thing to do, that's all.

The bird's profile vanished as it faced him.

'I see you down there,' came a harsh voice. 'I see you down there but I'll let you go for now, blat. You're brave and strong, rare qualities in a blat, and perhaps one day you'll be a great warrior. But remember, I and my fellow hawks own the sky. That moon up there, and every colour that glows in morning and night, belongs to us. If ever you come here again, I will catch you and take you to my lair in the crag, and feed you to my chicks who are hungrier than you could possibly believe.'

The hawk sighed. Perhaps, having remembered his chicks, he was having second thoughts about letting the blat go.

Pinguel stood up, missed his footing, and fell.

Through clumps of leaves, over and along branches, sliding down a trunk, laughing his deep-throated laugh at the thrill of it all, he rolled and tumbled until he came to a platform made of interwoven twigs outside a door with a sign over it that said 'Clerkwellstone Incorporated: Arch-Repairer and Orderer.' A scraping sound grew louder, then bristles scratched his arm, and a dry voice exclaimed:

'You! What in the world of branches are you doing here?'

An old blat with white hair and a rumpled, wine-coloured hat, climbed off the seat of his trundler, a machine with a rotating brush at the front for sweeping leaves and twig fragments from platforms.

Like all the blats from around here, Clerkwellstone had made the journey, several months ago, to inspect Pinguel, the foundling with the unblattish nose.

'*You.* Look at the mess you've made. And at your age, wandering about the forest alone. Ah well, I suppose it's the times we live in. The babies of today . . .' He shook his head, clucked his tongue, and carried Pinguel into his repairers' den.

Yet again, Pinguel found himself staring in wonder.

Clerkwellstone was famous among blats for being an arch-repairer so dedicated to his craft that he had no time even for golf. Seventy-two (eighteen on each wall) tiny, gas powered lights illuminated shelves upon which rested mechanical devices, mainly fragments and parts, some larger than Pinguel himself, others no bigger than the tip of the baby's little finger.

'No, no,' Clerkwellstone muttered as Pinguel struggled to get at these. 'Not for you. I'm telephoning your father, to get you out of here.' He brought his face closer to the baby's. 'Most of these objects are dangerous in the wrong hands. You have to understand them, to use them properly. My, you are strong.' He stated this flatly, without admiration. 'Maybe you'll grow up to be one of those brainless warriors. Or a golf player good at hitting a ball five hundred yards but who understands nothing about machinery. Hmph!'

As he looked up Cliffkin's number in the phone book, he went on:

'Or you'll become a sorcerer, like your father. Yes, we studied together, Cliffkin and I, though in different faculties.' He paused, finger on the number he wanted.

'As for sorcery,' Clerkwellstone continued, 'never had much time for it. Want to know why?' He spoke to the baby just as if Pinguel could understand every word he said. Pinguel liked this, so remained silent. 'Because of its uncertainty. With sorcery, you never know exactly where you are. Anything can happen. It's like, well, it's like riding on a wolf's back. You might get where you want to go, fast, but it isn't what I would call *safe*. But with machinery' — he gestured at the shelves of brightly lit agglomerations of metal — 'I know where I am. All a matter of cause and effect. Cliffkin, hello, is that you?'

With a sharp hiss, steam escaped from the side of the phone. 'Excuse me.' Clerkwellstone grabbed a wrench, and tightened a brass bolt. 'There we are. Madam Mambrol? Yes, no need to worry. Please, calm down. I have him here. Yes, he's perfectly all right.'

He glanced at Pinguel to make sure that this was true. 'Has some leaves in his hair, that's all. Do you want me to ...? No, all right. I'll keep him here then. Yes, I'll keep an eye on him.'

So Clerkwellstone hung up and, with a regretful glance at the mess of leaves and twigs on his platform, impossible to clean up with a baby in his arms, he sank into a deep armchair to await the arrival of Madam Mambrol. Resting the baby on his knees, the arch-repairer found himself wondering what life might have been like if someone had abandoned a baby in the fork of a nearby tree and *he* had been the one to find it. He thought of his occasional gusts of loneliness, most acute in the early evening when he put away his tools for the day, and sighed.

SEVEN ~~~

The next morning a storm was gathering. A cold haze chased leaves through the forest, and flashes of lightning lit up Pinguel's fingers as he struggled to open the window to find out if the red sky was still there, and if he could learn anything of his friends Silver Face and Peter Hawk. Cliffkin was asleep. Unable to open the window, the toddler staggered (he had only learned to walk yesterday, after all) to the bookshelves, and climbed until he came to a row of smooth, honey-coloured things.

Inside the piece that he was holding was a spider with a fat, hairy body and grasping legs.

He dropped it, not knowing why his hand had gone suddenly cold. Further along was a glass case containing what might have been half of a miniature, golden egg.

'For the Forest's sake, Pinguel!' cried Cliffkin, who had been woken by the lump of amber clunking onto the shelf.

Strong hands grasped the baby, who struggled. 'What were you reaching for? Ah, the Ant Bell. I'm not surprised, not a bit surprised.'

Cliffkin picked the bell off the bookcase and, careful not to trip over the trailing edge of his nightgown, sat in an armchair with Pinguel in his lap and the Ant Bell safely at the end of his arm, out of the baby's reach.

'Can I bring it closer, Pinguel, and you won't grab for it?'

The baby blinked at the glittering gold.

'One day,' Cliffkin explained, 'this will be yours. I only hope that you never have to pull out the tangle of wire inside. See? Gently soldered, but one firm pull should do it. Only in the direst, deepest, most dreadful and horrifying emergency should it be rung.' The sorcerer's soft voice gave these dramatic words a musical sound. They might have been part of a song.

'Oh Pinguel, what *are* you going to be when you grow up?'

What else had the owl, Sog, said?

He'll be blat-sized, but that's about all he'll have in common with blats, I think.

And now, with Pinguel on his lap, Cliffkin remembered something else the owl had told him.

You were chosen, Cliffkin. Yes, you were. You specifically. Not by me, but by Pinguel's mother. Your fame has spread further than you think. Enough, now. I cannot betray my secrets.

Chosen? Fame? It was bewildering.

'Ah, Pinguel. Mysteries. Well, they'll either become plain to us or they won't. Either way, we'll go on living, and getting to know one another.'

Pinguel's eyes widened, and he opened his mouth. He took a deep breath:

'What ith mythtery ith?' he asked in a husky voice.

EIGHT ~~~

Blats *never* spoke before the age of two.

Cliffkin stared, and felt a touch frightened by the baby on his knees. Then he felt again the strong emotion of yesterday, when he had first heard that Pinguel was safe at Clerkwellstone's place, and not eaten by wolves on the forest floor.

Once Pinguel had started to talk, he rarely stopped. One of his first questions, directed to Madam the next evening (over a dinner of roasted barley scones with a sauce made from tomatoes and cucumber), was:

'Are you mother mine?'

As he tilted his head to hear the answer, his long black hair fell half across his face, covering one eye.

During his eight months as a baby he had stored up many words, but without learning how to put them in the correct order. His voice was deep, as though hoarse from too much shouting. He had trouble saying 's'.

'Am I your mother?' repeated Madam. 'No, I am not.'

Pinguel folded his babyish arms. 'Mother, mine where ith?' He glanced around as though half expecting to make out a woman in the shadows.

'Your mother...' Cliffkin began. 'Your mother...'

'Another scone?' Madam offered.

The baby frowned. '*Mother?*'

Cliffkin took a deep breath.

'Your mother died soon after you were born. She left you with me to look after you.'

Except for the faint sound of blats singing in a nearby tree, and of a cable car rattling in the distance, silence filled Madam's dining room.

'Look after you? Mother,' Pinguel repeated. 'And Peter Hawk?'

'What?'

Pinguel pointed to the ceiling. 'Up with and play Pinguel.'

'Peter Hawk. Yes...' Madam hastened to fill the silence. 'I'll tell you a story about him tomorrow night, during your father's Magic Time. Ogren will be there, as well as your other friends: Barstow, Confail, Masty...'

'Magic Time?' Pinguel turned to Cliffkin.

'Yes.' The old blat was nodding. 'That's why you spend every Thursday night, eight until ten, with Madam. Every sorcerer, at least once a week, needs a couple of hours alone to practise and refine his art.'

NINE ~~~

At ten months old, Pinguel could no longer be called a baby. In two months he had learned to walk and even to run with a confidence that would have been impossible for a blat of his age. And his talking had improved. He had discovered the letter 's', and how to order words into sentences, though he had kept his distinctive, deepish voice.

Who, what, was he? wondered the blats of Deep Forest. Some were a little frightened of the talkative baby, but all were curious. Pinguel grew used to being stared at, and to blats taking a half, or even a whole step back when they first encountered him. He came to think it normal that no one but Cliffkin or Madam should accept him without this initial movement away.

Cliffkin held Pinguel close to his chest, and jumped into the trees.

The old sorcerer's mind was on his own thoughts, or he would have noticed something especially strange, tonight, about the toddler in his arms: Pinguel was paying extra-close attention to his surroundings. He watched each branch and bark handhold that Cliffkin used. He observed the other blats, all around, who greeted his father. There was Sentora, a woman who grew strawberries on an upper platform, carrying a length of hosepipe along a branch. Brafstoll, the miller, standing at his front door, sending up puffs of flour as he clapped his hands. Always after a day's work he stepped out to have a look at the world before going back for a wash, then down to the tavern for a size 12 (the largest) mug of honey ale.

Pinguel noticed every detail.

At least fifty toddlers and small children, and half as many adult blats, were crowded together on Madam's broad verandah. On the railing that went all around, as wide as a kitchen bench-top, Madam and the parents had positioned fruit, drinks and plates of biscuits and cake.

Shadows haunted the spaces between branches and trees. Pinguel thought he glimpsed a flickering, yellow light. Yes, it was the lantern over the doorway of Strolgo's warrior barracks, three trees distant.

Ogren crawled to Pinguel.

'Hello.' Pinguel took the toddler's hand, and they sat down at the back while Cliffkin both greeted and farewelled Madam and the other blats. Tonight was his Magic Time, the one night of the week that he spent alone.

Madam sat in an armchair, smoothed her dress, and opened a book.

'Shsh!' commanded two or three adults.

The smaller children, as usual, imitated this noise, and it was some seconds before the general hissing died away.

Pinguel watched carefully. Madam's hair was thick, like a tangle of fine wool. She wore a hat of the same dark green as her dress, with a feather curling from the band. Before beginning to read she brought out gold-rimmed spectacles and balanced them on her nose. When she looked up from her book, she peered over these rather than through them.

'Thank you for coming. Tonight I am going to read to you from the Blat Annals.'

The older blat children put their arms around their knees and hoped desperately for one of the old stories about a battle, or a journey that would seem hopeless at the start but which blats would complete due to their superior courage.

Madam caught Pinguel's eye, smiled, and began:

'Some say that blats are descended, so many years ago that it would be impossible to count them, from a flock of forest birds that is now extinct.'

A few of the older children laughed. The idea of it! For blats to be related to those squawking creatures!

'But certain it is,' Madam proceeded, shadows masking

her eyes as she looked down at the book, 'that hundreds of years ago, when the forest was young and many of the trees in which we now live were brightest green, and still growing, certain it is that in those days the relations between blats and birds were more cordial than they are now. *Archaeologists'* — Madam looked up, fixing everyone with this impressive word — 'who learn about the past by studying its ruins and remains, have discovered that many old cups and bowls are made of a type of glass that the blats in this forest lack the materials to create. Birds, they believe, brought these objects here from far places as part of a system of trade.'

Children settled deeper into the cushions as Madam's voice cradled them into those mysterious past days, when blats had traded with birds and the forest was brightest green. Turned down low, the lanterns gave out a deep and thoughtful light.

Pinguel pushed himself a little back.

'And *wolves!*' The word startled everyone, and was followed by a murmur of throat clearing and whispers as children and adults sat up straighter to hear what would come next.

'Wolves. What do the Annals say of them? *Blats rode on their backs in those far-off days!*

'Yes,' Madam nodded, replying to looks of disbelief, 'ask Professor Sumpter, the famous archaeologist, who spends his days among ancient things dug up by miners in their search for metal ores, or found by warriors in their patrols through far and deserted trees. He will show you a vase, pieced together out of shattered fragments, on which is pictured a blat riding on the back of a wolf.'

Pinguel shifted right back into the shadows.

'During these far-off times,' Madam read out, 'there lived a blat called Camster, who disliked soap, and preferred dirt ...'

Moving with a precision and swiftness unknown to blats of his age, Pinguel pulled himself onto the verandah railing.

Crouched down, he grabbed a branch and allowed it to take his weight gradually enough to stop the leaves from making a noise. Then he swung forward until his feet found another branch. He did this several times, then straightened, and looked back.

Madam Mambrol's verandah was an island of light in an ocean of dark, twisting shapes.

Pinguel swung through the forest as he had never done by himself before.

The trick (he had learned, from watching his father) was to think two branches ahead, no more and no less: the one you are travelling to, and the one after that. Think any further, and you risk not seeing the branch you are heading for; not far enough, and you find yourself hanging by both hands without a follow-up.

Pinguel found that trees contained surprises. The way twigs scratched at his arms and face, for instance (because he was travelling by a rarely used path). Another was speed: he had felt it with Cliffkin, but it seemed much faster now.

He was heading for his own house, Number 14, Drimsen Pallisades. Ever since Pinguel could remember, he had had to leave on Thursday nights, usually for Madam's place, so that his father could have his solitary Magic Time.

'Sorcerers must keep on learning,' Cliffkin had explained, 'however old they are. Otherwise their brains rust, or — if you prefer — fill with weeds.'

Yet Pinguel had noticed, in his father's eyes, the shadow of a thought kept back. He suspected that Cliffkin was not telling the whole truth.

He crept across the verandah, then peered through the window of the bed-sitting room.

Empty.

Next along was his father's study.

Careful to take silent breaths, and conscious of the beating of his own heart, he crouched beneath the window and slowly, slowly, straightened. He hoped to discover the mystery of his father's sorcery, to learn why it was that blats went to him for advice, and left soothed; why blats, even Pinguel himself, couldn't help feeling a kind of strength within the old blat. Did Cliffkin, on Thursday evenings, summon up monsters from the depths of the tree, from the passages that led to the abandoned mineshaft far below, to tell him their secrets?

'It's complicated. I'll tell you one day, I promise, when there's time,' was all Cliffkin would say.

Pinguel's eyes reached the level of the window.

His father was sitting at a desk. He raised to his mouth something golden and glistening at the end of a fork. Before him stood a plate of pancakes and syrup. He was reading a book. He finished the pancakes, left the room, and returned with more. Pinguel narrowed his eyes with impatience. If something interesting didn't happen soon, he would go back to Madam's verandah.

When he had finished eating, Cliffkin used a key to open one of his many desk drawers. He took out a metal box, and, with another key from the same ring, unlocked it.

This was better.

Standing as high as he could, Pinguel still couldn't make out what was inside. Cliffkin reached in with both hands and lifted out an object that it took Pinguel a couple of seconds (which seemed a long time) to realise was a tiny bed, hardly longer than the sorcerer's outstretched hand. He placed this on the desk, and only now did the boy notice a golden head on the pillow.

Ands someone was under the bedcovers.

Pinguel held his breath. From the de Wartons' place, next door, came laughter, a door shutting, and footsteps on the verandah. Pinguel looked over his shoulder and saw the face of the elder de Warton, Alex, flare orange as he puffed on his pipe.

Pinguel prayed that Alex wouldn't spot him. He was too engrossed in what he was seeing to move away.

The tiny, golden-haired figure stirred, stretched out both arms, and sat on the edge of the bed. She was wearing a long, white nightdress. Swinging her legs back and forth, she stretched her arms again and said something that Pinguel didn't hear.

Cliffkin reached again into the drawer and brought out another box, this time wooden. He inserted a key and slowly, slowly, opened it into two halves, each with a pattern of gold and black squares: a chessboard. (Cliffkin had taught Pinguel to play, though had never used this set.)

The tiny woman (no taller than a blat's thumb) went over to Cliffkin's plate, dipped a fingertip in the syrup, and licked it.

Cliffkin pulled back the lids of the board's two side-compartments, but made no move to take out any of the pieces. As the woman this time dipped all her fingers into the syrup and one by one licked them, he looked on, head tilted at an angle that expressed both admiration and concern.

A hand, then an arm, stuck up from a compartment. A pointed silver helmet arose at an angle on a yawning man's face. He straightened the helmet, stroked a pointy beard, climbed to the board, took a deep breath, and stood to attention, face solemn, on a pawn square.

Two white horses, each with a silver-helmeted warrior on its back, bounded from one compartment; two black ones from the other. A man in long robes, wearing a golden crown, helped up a woman, also wearing a crown. Then came more of the helmeted men, and four taller figures wearing hoods, two heavily armoured warriors ... until all the living pieces of the chessboard were in position.

The pawns were a little shorter than the golden-haired woman, the royal pieces only half a head taller.

The woman moved to side of the board, sat on the edge of a book, and spoke.

A pawn marched forward, and halted after two squares. In obedience to a command from Cliffkin, the opposite pawn marched up. The first pawn grinned and muttered something, whereupon all the pieces laughed and stood at ease. A castle sat down to adjust a side-strap of his sandal. From beneath his robe, a bishop took out a mirror and pair of scissors, and began to trim his beard.

Pinguel leapt into darkness, and raced through the forest.

Who were the golden-haired woman and the chess people?

He would read his father's books. Perhaps they would tell him.

Peering over the Blat Annals, pretending to be absorbed only in what she was reading, Madam noticed Pinguel's return and found herself hoping with all her heart that she would live for long enough to see what exactly became of this strange non-blat.

TEN ~~~

so Pinguel taught himself to read, and the more he read, the faster he became at it. Over the next weeks, then months — three, four, five months — he read book after book, sometimes in bed, sometimes sprawled on Cliffkin's armchair, sometimes lying on the rug. He read all the eighteen volumes of the Blat Annals, then turned to books of sorcery. He learned that anything could be changed into anything, or summoned from anywhere, but only if many conditions were met. And these depended on so many details, such as where you happened to be, the temperature of the air, your mood, and so on, that, in the words of one author, 'Magic is best left alone by all except those fine minds capable of remembering many details and of tolerating frequent disappointments.'

Both Cliffkin and Madam tried to get Pinguel to play outside, on the platform.

'There's much more to life ...' Cliffkin began, one night when a high wind made the forest sound as if it was full of crashing ocean waves. 'Please, Pinguel, there's *much* more to life than can be found in all the books ever written. You don't play any more. What is it? What's wrong?'

The sorcerer had been alarmed to notice, all of a sudden, how thin the boy had become. Not yet two years old, he should have still had much of his baby plumpness, yet here he was with cheeks sunken and eyes ringed with shadow. Except for his shoulder-length black hair he might have been an old blat rather than a toddler.

He answered in his distinctive, husky voice:

'Yes, father, I know.'

'Do you? Then spend some time outside! Let's go, now, and play golf. I know a lovely course not far away, where the moss of the fairways is deep green, and on windy days like this the ball whirls at speeds of over a hundred miles an hour. Highly convenient' — he lowered his voice — 'if you're not especially expert at driving.'

Pinguel continued to stare at his father. He had learned a great deal, but nothing to explain the golden-haired girl or the living chess pieces. And he felt strongly that he couldn't just come out and ask about these things and confess that he had spied on him.

'Yes.' He jumped up. 'Golf. I want to learn about it. And I want to go to school too. Can I start tomorrow? I know I'm young, but I think I'm ready for it.'

'Of course you are,' Cliffkin answered, so relieved at Pinguel's enthusiasm that for the moment he hardly knew what he was saying. 'I'll talk to Clew, the headmaster. Come, though, let's play. We can talk as we go. The best thing about golf is that it allows for much talking.'

So they went to one of the forest's best-known golf shops, owned by Emma Bardle. A net made of wire stood in a corner, each strand attached to the sensors of a steam-driven pressure gauge. Miss Bardle handed Pinguel a tiny driving wood. An aunt of Finquay, the mayor, was trying on a pair of tasselled golf shoes at the far end of the store.

'You're extremely young,' Miss Bardle said, giving Cliffkin a disapproving look. Still, it would be a shame to turn away a paying customer.

'I think he'll manage,' put in Cliffkin, as Miss Bardle pointed a remote control unit at a television set behind the net. The screen flashed into a picture of a moss-covered fairway curving and dipping between and around branches and finishing with a distant white flag.

'Now,' Miss Bardle began to explain, 'this will give us an idea of the weight and length of the club that you require, little one. Please hit the ball as hard as you can, pretending that the net isn't there, and aim for the white flag. The net will catch the ball and measure the direction and speed of your drive. And don't worry' — she gave Cliffkin another reproachful look — 'don't worry if you fail to hit the ball, or if it only rolls along the floor. Do you understand me?'

'I understand,' Pinguel answered.

'Go ahead then.' Miss Bardle sighed.

Even the smallest club looked too big in Pinguel's hands. He held it awkwardly and murmured:

'As hard as possible? All right then.'

He brought the club past his shoulder and behind his head in the fashion favoured by the greatest golf masters, then flashed it down.

The club moved so amazingly quickly that streaks of fire appeared around it, as with a spacecraft entering the earth's atmosphere. It smashed into the ball at a colossal speed and sent it tearing through the wire net built to withstand the most powerful strokes, then, with a loud explosion, smashed through the television screen, all the machinery behind it, and clean through the wall of the shop ... until it disintegrated with an earth-shuddering explosion against a tree trunk, narrowly missing a cable car full of golfers returning from the course and on their way to the famous Bardle tearooms.

Miss Bardle stared. The mayor's aunt stared.

Cliffkin had to use every scrap of his most persuasive sorcerer's arts.

'*A defective ball!*' he proclaimed, giving Miss Bardle a reassuring touch on the shoulder, then hopping across opened shoe boxes to do the same for Emsy Finquay.

'One in a million,' he elaborated, when he had given them both his sorcerer's touch. 'And when you take into account' — he was fingering a strand of broken wire — 'a net weakened by defective soldering, and' — he pointed to the shattered, smoking TV screen — 'glass with a quite imperceptible crack across it, about to fall to pieces anyway, well, we should have foreseen this, shouldn't we?'

Cliffkin was a truly persuasive sorcerer.

'Defective wire...' Miss Bardle murmured, touching a strand of the torn metal. 'I'll have to get in touch with the manufacturer.'

'That could have been dangerous, you know,' agreed the mayor's aunt, returning to her examination of golfing shoes.

'You must *never* do that again,' Cliffkin warned his son when they were on the fairway. He took several deep breaths, closed his eyes, opened them, swung back his club and hit a ball straight into a pipe, one of five in front of him. A red circle, activated by a wire inside, rose above the opening: '3', it said.

'Number three, not bad. Your shot. Do you understand me, Pinguel? Of course you do. I apologise. I'm exhausted from dealing with those women. But how can you be so strong? Where' — he mused to himself — 'where could you have got such strength? But Pinguel,' he shrugged to make himself more alert, 'the one thing, perhaps, that you don't understand, is how fearful and nervous blats can be. And we don't want them frightened of you, do we? Then you'd be all alone. They'd avoid you, and *everyone* would suffer.'

'Yes, father. It's just that she seemed so certain that I'd be a hopeless hitter.'

'You proved her wrong then, didn't you? But remember: keep your strength a secret from blats, or you'll lose their company, and, worse for them, they'll lose yours.'

ELEVEN ～～

The next day, Cliffkin visited the headmaster of the local school, and, using only a touch of sorcerer's persuasiveness, arranged for Pinguel to sit the entrance exam.

The school occupied three large trees, with the playground a vast platform that joined them together. A crowd of blat schoolchildren, swinging bags and shouting at one another, were pouring from a cable car in through the main gates. Pinguel took the test at a desk in a corner of the headmaster's study.

Father and son waited in a hallway full of echoing school sounds as a teacher marked the test.

'Congratulations,' boomed the headmaster. Although a little pompous, he was a kindly man, and was genuinely pleased that Pinguel had done well. 'A brilliant performance. Why don't you begin next week? A few mistakes, but, never mind, that's why you'll be coming to school: to learn!'

Earlier, Cliffkin had warned: 'Don't do too well. Get at least three questions wrong, or the headmaster will be shocked.'

Deep in the middle of that night, when all the animals in the forest, except for prowling wolves and a certain scholarly owl, were fast asleep, Pinguel woke up.

The clock was ticking, and the sound of his father's slow, sleepful breathing came from across the room.

Pinguel crept to where Cliffkin's trousers lay across a chair, and reached into the pockets for keys. He took these out, crossed the room, and silently opened and closed behind him the study door. The room was dark, but Pinguel knew to stand still and allow his eyes to adjust.

He soon made out the desk with its locked drawers. From the window came moonlight so pale that it hardly existed. Silver Face, Pinguel thought to himself as he went to the desk. From his reading he knew that Silver Face was only the moon, a lifeless rock in empty space. He went to turn on the lamp over Cliffkin's desk but remembered first to grab two cushions from an armchair and put them against the bottom of the door to prevent the light from showing.

He tried one key after another until he unlocked the drawer that, from the window, he had seen Cliffkin open. Except for the metal box and a chess set it was empty.

He took out the metal box and placed it gently on the desk. There were five keys on Cliffkin's ring, but only one the right size for the box.

'Stop,' he told himself.

He was breathing quickly, as though he had just this moment finished swinging through trees.

He put the key in the hole, and turned it.

As he raised the lid, his heart climbed in his chest, and he almost shouted with delight.

There she lay in her tiny bed, fast asleep.

Light fell across the purple blanket, with the sheet turned over the top of it. Beside the bed was a table with a red-shaded lamp. The box-room also contained a wardrobe and — Pinguel was astonished to see — a set of blat-sized knitting needles on the floor. The lamplight shone onto his smiling face, his eyes wide open to absorb as much of this sight as possible. So, such a thing as this *did* exist. That was what he had wanted to discover for certain.

Truly the world was full of mysteries.

He was about to close the lid of the box when the girl sat up. She pushed her golden hair back, and stared at Pinguel.

'No, don't be frightened,' the boy whispered.

Her eyes were open wide, and she raised her hands as though to push Pinguel away, but instead brought them to her throat.

'Cliffkin!' she whispered in a choking voice, before falling back on the bed, hands still at her throat.

'No,' Pinguel whispered, then shouted: 'No!'

His hands hovered helplessly over the box. He wanted to pick her up, do something that would make her all right, but had no idea what.

Pushing the cushions, the door behind him opened and Cliffkin appeared. He stood there, one hand rubbing an eye.

'What ...?' he murmured until he saw the box with its lid open.

'Quick!' Pinguel shouted. 'She's...' He couldn't bring himself to say 'dying', but that's what he feared.

'Get some syrup!' Cliffkin commanded. 'The honey syrup from the middle shelf in the kitchen, as fast as you can.'

Pinguel ran. When he returned, his father was holding the girl in one hand while stroking her head with a fingertip. When Pinguel had set the jar down on the table, Cliffkin dipped his fingertip into the syrup, then touched it to the girl's pale lips.

Although sunk in self-disgust, in a longing somehow to punish himself for the damage that he had done, Pinguel couldn't help noticing how lovely she was. She reminded him of his first sight of the moon; it had looked beautifully cold after the easy closeness of the trees.

The drops of syrup rested on her lips.

Cliffkin shook, and Pinguel saw tears in his father's eyes.

'No,' he muttered, as the horror of what was happening came over him.

Then the girl opened her mouth, slightly.

'Shsh!' Cliffkin commanded.

The drop of syrup grew smaller, then her tiny, pink tongue came out and licked more into her mouth.

Pinguel's mind felt blank. Hopefulness and despair had concelled each other out, leaving nothing behind.

Then the drop of syrup vanished, and the girl opened her eyes. She stared from Cliffkin to Pinguel, then whispered, just loud enough for the blat and his son to hear:

'My, this is a surprise.'

It was the middle of the night and all the blats of Deep Forest, except for one, were asleep.

'I spied on you through the window,' Pinguel confessed to both the girl, now sitting up in bed, arms around knees, and to Cliffkin. 'Then, then . . .'

'And then you had to know, so you did all that reading, learning in a few months more than most blats do in their whole lives, but without discovering the secret of Faringaria.

'Well, I'm not surprised, because it isn't in any book in the world. No, stop apologising, please. It was partly my fault for not remembering to close the shutters. But then, if I'd been in the habit of doing that, I would never have found you, would I? No, allow me to finish. You should have asked me. I would have told you. I can trust you to keep a secret, I know. I suppose it's just that secrets have become a great habit with me, over the years.'

The girl was watching. Cliffkin turned to her: 'Do you want to go back to sleep, Faringaria?'

'I suppose I should. Thank you. Goodnight, Cliffkin. And Pinguel, goodnight. I'll see you both again soon.'

Cliffkin waited until she was comfortably in her bed, then closed the lid. There were no airholes. So was she a living creature, or not?

'In my youth,' Cliffkin began, 'which is longer ago than you might suppose, I wandered far and wide through Deep Forest. I went around Dragon's Tooth and all the way to the foothills of the Cold Mountains. In the other direction I explored both banks of the River Docker in search of medicinal herbs for my teacher, Fomsaxtil, perhaps the greatest sorcerer blats have ever had. He lived by himself, not far from the river. Everyone feared him. They went to him, of course, in times of need — illness and suchlike — and he would help them, but they feared his power.

'One day I was hanging upside down from a branch over the river, reaching for a bunch of cragwort berries. These — perhaps I don't need to tell you after all your reading — are invaluable for curing earache. I was about to grab them, when there was such a barking as I had never in all my life heard. So I did what all good blats should do when confronted with something strange and terrifying: I froze, upside down, hand still outstretched for the berries, and tried to make myself as invisible as I could.

'On the opposite bank eight wolves were pulling a chariot. They were *racing* along, ears pressed back, straining for maximum speed. Raising a whip high to goad the wolves to even greater efforts was a creature a good deal taller than the tallest human, but one that apart from having a head, two arms, and two legs, bore no resemblance to any living creature.

'It was made of dark metal. Its fingers were claws, and as it turned this way and that, searching, a beam of light came from a slit across its face. Armour ... yes, it was a knight in armour, or — as I found out later — a Knight of

53

Work. The rumbling of the chariot's wheels over roots and rocks filled the forest and, with the barking of the wolves, was enough to make the river sink fearfully between its banks.

'Then came more chariots, and more and more. I closed my eyes, held my breath, and prayed for them not to see me.

'Chariots rumbled to the banks, and their riders examined the water. The knights lashed the surface with whips. Then they sped on, and the river almost stopped flowing, so humiliated was it by this treatment.

'Over near the far bank bare toes, terribly pale, broke the surface. V-shaped ripples trailed from a single reed. The reed was moving through the water. Then a head appeared — but one, I confess, such as I had never seen. Bald except for a wisp of hair plastered across, only one eye blinking with the greatest possible wariness, while the other wasn't closed, it was absent, and water dribbled from its empty socket. Then I noticed other reeds, and other hands and feet, shoulders and arms, and finally heads, breaking the surface. And all the heads were ugly; there's no other word for it, my dear Pinguel, no other word. They were the sorts of heads that are never shown on TV, but exist all the same: ones with the nose spread halfway across the face, without proper chins, sporting ears that stick madly out, like batwings, or with wiry hair that stands up straight like the bristles on a brush. Ugly heads, in short, and as these people climbed out on my side of the bank, and whispered to one another, and helped each other over the slippery mud, I saw that their bodies, too, were ugly. Some hunchbacked, others hugely fat, some with long, clownlike feet, others possessing hands and arms that hung, ape-like. None were graceful, none looked like the pictures of blats and people in storybooks or on TV. And they were covered in mud, slime, and green mould and algae. They stood not far from the tree, close enough for me to hear them talk. There were seventeen of them.

'The first to come from the water, the one-eyed one, was a woman, and appeared to be their leader. She looked around and — I was almost certain — caught sight of me. But she pretended that she had seen nothing.

'She spoke to a short, bowed-over man.

'"Well, Glaffer, we've eluded them. They didn't want to get their beautiful armour wet, did they?"

'"No indeed," Glaffer laughed, stamping his feet to get the water out of his boots. "But now we're in Wolf Forest, and what do you propose to do about that, oh Queen?"

'"Ah yes." The Queen blinked her single eye. "We have escaped from the cauldron, onto the coals. Unless ... unless ..." And then she turned that eye on me, on young Cliffkin, still hanging by his knees, upside down, and said:

'"Unless this little fellow, a blat if I'm not mistaken, can help us. No, no, don't worry" — she hastened to reassure me — "we mean you no harm. We won't chase you if you run away. We couldn't if we tried; you're so fast through the trees. But it's known to a few, to the learned among us, that blats live here, and that Blat Magic is a force to be reckoned with. Here, young blat, let me help you down. There we are. See? I place you on the ground, and you are free to go, or to swing through the trees with your blat swiftness."

'I stood before them, my mouth open. I was young, as I've told you. I had no presence of mind. Then I heard the chariots. Maybe it was just a breeze, bringing back some of their noise, or maybe they had turned and were coming towards us. To make matters worse, we were on the ground. I suddenly remembered this. The *ground*: the least safe place in the world for a blat. Surely the wolves would by now have smelt us out.

'Despite all the rush, and my surprise, I had time to feel sorry for these people. They stood helpless before me, nowhere to go. They were ugly, and — from the ragged clothes and rough boots, many with the leather splitting or curling away from the sole — poor too. Who in the world would want such people, except as slaves, as living machines?

'"Come with me," I said. I led them away from the river, towards my master Fomsaxtil's tree. They climbed with great difficulty, with much noise from their huffing and puffing and breaking of the branches that would not take their weight.

'When only one or two were off the ground, and helping the others up, Fomsaxtil came out and leaned over the verandah.

'"By uppermost branches, Cliffkin, what have you done?"

'No time for explanations. The wizard and I directed the fugitives to the branches and platforms around his quarters. Lucky he lived apart from other blats, or the whole forest would have known what was happening.

'"We cannot go back," stated their leader, the one-eyed woman. "We know we are doomed. There is no way out of the forest. There are the Cold Mountains, which no one has ever crossed, and in the other direction lie the lands from which we are fleeing. Yes" — she lowered her head for hardly a moment, then raised it in pride — "I can see, blat, that you are wise enough, and learned enough, to know who we are."

'"We are the lowest, the least worthy, the ones not wanted anywhere except for dangerous, boring or filthy tasks. We are slaves, in all but name. We plotted among ourselves to save our money, to break free from work, but of course this was not allowed, so they hunted us in their chariots; it was a sport to them, and now here we are."

'To my enormous surprise, she laughed, and her companions, her followers, laughed with her. They patted one another's shoulders, and squeezed each other's hands, and as they settled more easily on their branches, and on the woven platforms, I saw what it was. They had each other; that was the thing. They weren't lonely. And believe me, that is no small achievement.

'If only you could have seen Fomsaxtil! What a wizard! Ah, Pinguel, that old man taught me all I know, and more. He had a pale old face as thin and wrinkled as a twisted piece of paper. His fingers trembled from sheer age, and on each one he wore either an emerald or a ruby ring. Not for decoration, no, although he did love the look of them. They helped him to direct some of his strangest spells. He spoke in a voice not unlike yours — a little deeper than the average.

'"Well," he smiled, "how fond are you of things that you can't decide for yourselves, eh?"

'They looked at him, mystified.

'"I mean things such as your charming looks, your size, the colour of your hair? How would you feel about losing these things forever? Wait, answer me this: How is my old friend Peregrine, and his Order of Stowaways? Do you know of them? You are just the types, if I am not mistaken, to have done so."

'And Fomsaxtil leaned forward, wrinkled old face eager with curiosity, and the rings on his fingers sparkled with their jewelled lights.

'"We were looking for him, O wise one," said the woman with only one eye. This eye had widened with surprise at the name of Peregrine. "But we didn't find him. We searched everywhere, with no luck."

'"Yes ..." The wizard sighed. "A hard wizard to find. Not in this forest. No, you won't find him here. Nearer the coast, I think, these days, but you can't travel there from here. Did you know that?"

'The woman gave a single nod, waiting for Fomsaxtil to go on.

'I had got over my surprise enough to wonder what would happen next. Now and then a breeze carried the barking of wolves into our midst. What could possibly be done, by blats, for these giants?

'But Fomsaxtil didn't seem worried by this. I had never seen him quite so unworried, in fact. He pulled an armchair out, and sat down. The humans, for that is what they were, were balancing uncomfortably among the branches. It was their first time, that was obvious, in trees.

'"But I remember Peregrine well," Fomsaxtil went on. "One of those rare types who, for an unknown reason, never grow old. I remember him in the days when he used to sit with his feet on his windowsill, reading and keeping an eye on the weather. In those days he had a dragon called Tinderwell, who used to try to persuade him to take a more active interest in the world. That was long before he formed the Order of Stowaways, of course."

'"But sitting around here, talking over old times, isn't getting us far, is it? You haven't answered my question. Are you attached to your appearance? Would any of you object to" — he held up one hand, as though grasping something invisible, and his rings sparkled — "a *permanent change*?"

'The woman, obviously their leader, smiled. Then the others looked at one another. In no way were they ashamed of their looks. They didn't despise one another, let alone themselves, on the stupid ground of physical appearance. And yet in this serious time, with hope all but extinguished, they would not object to a change.

'"Good!" cried Fomsaxtil. "You are proud, but not too proud. Stubborn, but not to the point of self-ruination. Good. Wait here. Back in a moment. Come inside, Cliffkin. Here's a chance for you to learn something."'

Cliffkin ran his fingertips all the way down, and back up again, one of the two rows of drawers that went all the way from the top of his desk to the floor. 'And here is where you learn something too, Pinguel. Not that you will ever become a sorcerer. No, you have more important work to do. Here, though, is where you learn a taste of the power, but also of the weakness, of Blat Magic.'

The night was silent except for the secretive tick of the clock in the next room. Cliffkin folded his arms, and his face took on a composed look that Pinguel could not remember having seen before. The desk drawers were closed. There were one, two ... twelve on each side.

Inside one was a metal box with a miniature bedroom and a golden-haired girl, fast asleep, lips sticky with syrup.

'Blat magic deals in *little* things,' Cliffkin went on. 'That is what Fomsaxtil used to say. He took me into his house, that afternoon, and told me to fetch a box of toys from his wardrobe.'

'"These are important," he told me while the fugitives waited outside, uncomfortable on their branches, "because I used to play with them as a child. They made up my world then, and for Blat Magic, as I've told you many times, that is the single richest source of power: your private world. But we have to hurry. The wolves will have told the knights where the fugitives are. The knights are coming. We mustn't dither, or nothing will be able to help us. Come, you take the chessboard. I'll bring this metal box."

'He went to the railing of his verandah and addressed the humans.

('You haven't seen humans, Pinguel, so it might be hard for you to get a sense of how huge they are, compared to us. I tell you, though: the branches were bending under their weight. Big branches, thicker than a cable car! And their smell! Clothes filthy, and damp, and oozing with mud. It was lucky indeed that Fomsaxtil lived apart from other blats.')

'The old sorcerer held up the box and chessboard.

'"So you wish to hide, and do not mind a change of appearance?"

'The humans nodded.

'Now we could hear the barking of wolves.

'"You will enter a state of hibernation," the sorcerer explained, having to speak quickly now, "like the bears in the foothills of the Cold Mountains. You will come out from time to time — to eat, to play — but not permanently for many, many years, until things are safer, or until they are even more dangerous than now, and there is need of you. You will change your forms, but I cannot say exactly how. Smaller, smaller, you will be, otherwise how could we hide you? This may not be permanent, though, but the change of shape will be."

'"You will look different to the way you do now, and for all time!"

'The humans simply nodded. They were long past hope, you see. A few minutes ago they had believed themselves about to be eaten by wolves.

'So Fomsaxtil sat down in his armchair and proceeded to surprise everyone, including me, by opening the two boxes on the table, and pulling a tangle of knitting from a jacket pocket. The needles were golden, the wool all different colours. He sat down, hummed to himself, and began to knit.

'I feared that he had gone mad, I confess.

'Poor Fomsaxtil, I thought, and even poorer humans, now certain to be eaten up by wolves.

'Then the needles began to glow, and this glowing drained the light from the forest until the faces of the humans shone like moons in a midnight sky. And the wool ... Not ordinary wool, I can assure you of that. As the wizard knitted, getting faster and faster, the coloured strands spun increasingly into the sudden night, and curled themselves around the faces of the humans. And what colours! Deep, deep, as though each was burning in its own lovely fire. The strands tangled up the pale humans until all I could make of them were faces and hands.

'Fomsaxtil knitted so quickly that the green and red of his rings burned into the colours of the wool. The humans began to whirl around, eyes and mouths wide open with surprise, perhaps with pain, arms and hands stretched out in protest, but no, it was too late for that.

'They were stretched into ribbons, long and thin. They joined the wool, and Fomsaxtil's knitting, until finally he held up his hands, above his head, muttered a few words in Old Blat, and brought the needles down on the tops of the plain metal box and the chessboard.

'And now the night was empty and quiet.

'Later, of course, he showed me what was inside the containers: thirty-two living chess pieces, with Faringaria the Princess in the other. And indeed' — now Cliffkin's eyes had gone out of focus, as though he was straining to recall something that had happened a very long time ago — 'and indeed, this change truly caught the essential nature of these people. Faringaria really was a leader, a princess, and at least in the eyes of her people her beauty was complete, like that of the golden-haired Faringaria you saw this evening. And as for the others, each is different, with different strengths and failings, like the pieces in chess, but they all still look to Faringaria for leadership, even the kings and queens.

'They are weak in their hibernating state, and can only stand a certain amount of activity. Surprises put a great strain on them. That is why Faringaria, this evening, became so dangerously tired. They feed on liquid sugar, or syrup — Faringaria once a week, the others once a month. Without it they go deeper and deeper into hibernation. If this happens only Fomsaxtil's knitting needles can revive them. These are underneath Faringaria's bed, and her mattress is made of skeins of wool.

'It's late, but there's one more thing. You are not so young as you look, are you? Or should I say, you are older than your years. Anyway, I don't think you are too young for another surprise. Perhaps you have guessed it already, with your intelligence. Yes, I see that you have.'

Soon the sun would rise, but in these depths of Deep Forest it would remain dark for at least forty minutes after that. The only sign of dawn would come from the birds, the smaller ones twittering in the treetops, in search of insects to eat and dewdrops to sip, while the larger species — hawks and eagles — soared high in their ceaseless search for voles, rabbits and (although they found them so rarely nowadays that it was hardly a dim memory in the minds of the oldest of them) for blats.

'*I'm the same*,' Pinguel said. 'The same as Faringaria and the others. And...' he looked down at the other drawers of the desk.

He knew this from a coldness in the air of the room. He knew that his mother had fled into the forest, and that he had been left here. And he knew that he wasn't a blat.

Cliffkin smiled. 'Nearly, but not exactly.'

He proceeded to open the other desk drawers, and from these he took out other boxes: slender ones, like those that contain knives and forks as gifts, and plump ones such as might hold drinking mugs. Boxes with clasps on them, and keyholes; boxes with padlocks, and one (blue, with the picture of a unicorn carved into it) wrapped around with a chain. Twenty, thirty — no, about fifty little boxes in all, contained in the two columns of desk drawers that supported the sorcerer's desk.

'Yes, Pinguel,' Cliffkin went on, 'and they all contain humans and merryns who have fled into our forest and, as far as anyone else is concerned, have ceased to exist. There are five hundred and eighty-two of them here, and none had anywhere else to go. This room, this desk, was their last refuge. They aren't made to live in trees, like us, and the ground is too unsafe. As for the world beyond the forest...' Cliffkin had begun to replace the boxes in their drawers. 'It is harsh, Pinguel. It is not like Deep Forest is for blats. There is not room for everyone, out there.'

PART THREE

TWELVE ~~~

In autumn the trees of Deep Forest did not lose their leaves, but a chill came into the air and a real iciness into lower shadows. And on winter's coldest days a stillness emptied the air, and snow hurried to fill the vacuum.

During his first winter with Cliffkin, Pinguel watched the snowflakes, and decided that they were playing a desperate game of who could survive the longest among branches, twigs, leaves, cables and blat platforms.

Most astonishing were those that simply plummeted, straight down, through a tiny gap in the world. Pinguel watched the snowflakes each winter, and always wondered if any made it to the forest floor. Sometimes he followed them, but he never saw a snowflake get past the middle level of blat platforms.

Spring, summer, autumn and winter he went to school, and because there was nothing difficult about the work, and because he never felt that he really belonged in the playground games and conversations of his fellow students, he concentrated on golf. Although he never again hit the ball nearly as hard as he had in Miss Bardle's shop, he nevertheless acquired a reputation as a powerful hitter.

'Exceptionally strong for his age,' said his first golfing report, signed by Coach Wortle, 'though he could do with more accuracy. A little impulsive in his choice of club.'

Cliffkin had smiled at this. 'Yes, *impulsive*,' he had said to himself, one chilly winter's evening as snowflakes drifted past his eternally unshuttered window.

Cliffkin and Pinguel spent every Thursday night together in the sorcerer's study, and within a few months the boy knew all the tiny humans and merryns in the boxes in Cliffkin's desk drawers.

Most woke up sleepy and absent-minded when the lids of their boxes were raised. Some were peeved, even angry, to find themselves no longer asleep. A merryn who had once been old and lame (Cliffkin told Pinguel) but who now looked barely fifteen years old, would always grumble: 'So what is it now, eh? What's the fuss?'

Except for Faringaria, everyone shared their box with others. There were boxes not only of living chess pieces, but also of musicians complete with instruments, of acrobats in tights, with throwing pins, a ball and hoop, of actors who knew the lines of many human plays by heart, and were only too happy to give a performance, but the most common groups were soldiers: archers in bright tunics and bronze helmets; swordsmen who, as soon as their lid was raised, would begin to polish their blades; and even a squad of cavalry, who spent their waking time rubbing polish into bridles, saddles and girth straps, now and then raising their heads expectantly, as though listening for their horses, surely due any minute.

Pinguel thought of Faringaria as their leader, or at least as the one to whom they would turn for leadership when the time came for them to leave their boxes.

'Will that time ever come, father?' Pinguel asked one winter's day, when, although it was only two o'clock in the afternoon, there was hardly any light in the forest.

'Oh yes, one day. I think so.'

'And the Ant Bell...?' Pinguel began. Although he had asked the question many times, he couldn't help himself. He loved to hear the answer.

'And the Ant Bell. One day will someone take out the wire, and ring it? And what will happen then, do you think?'

Cliffkin would pause in whatever he was doing and look at a spot in space. 'Who will ring it? Why, it might be you, Pinguel. Would you like that?'

At first, Pinguel couldn't help exclaiming:

'Oh yes, I'd love to see what it does,' but as he grew older his replies changed until he found himself saying, from about the age of eight or nine:

'No, I don't want Deep Forest to change. I never want the blats to be in such great danger that the bell has to be rung.'

THIRTEEN ~~~

So Pinguel went to school, and played golf with his best friend, Ogren, and just as spring follows winter, and is sometimes hardly noticeable until it has turned the corner into summer (when suddenly there is light throughout the forest), so the years crept onward, one after the other.

Sometimes on a Saturday or Sunday afternoon, or on any day during the holidays, Pinguel would visit Madam, and read her legends, study the Annals, or just talk. Ever since discovering Faringaria he had not attended her Thursday nights, so he made up for it this way.

About once a month he visited Clerkwellstone, the arch-repairer who had found him on the day that he had learned to walk and climb (and fall), and together they would have cups of lemon-scented tea and discuss what each had been doing since their last meeting. Pinguel relished having an adult friend who wasn't (as he thought of Cliffkin and Madam) a relation. Clerkwellstone would take down bits of machinery and explain how they worked. His favourite phrase was: 'Strictly cause and effect.'

One cold afternoon at the end of the first week of his second year of high school, Pinguel was swinging through the trees towards Clerkwellstone's place, when he was overcome by an impulse to go further than he had ever gone before.

Overcome.

He thought of Clerkwellstone's machinery, and its 'strictly cause and effect'. Then why couldn't he be like that, and use his mind to control himself as strictly as a cable car's throttle, for instance, controls its pulley-motor?

He soon noticed a movement, and stood quite still, hands out to keep his balance. Then he saw the large eyes of the owl, Sog, who lived far away, and whom Pinguel had, from time to time, seen about the place watching him.

'An old family friend. Hates talking,' Cliffkin had explained when Pinguel was little. 'A scholar, addicted to being alone. Lives on potatoes, special potatoes, and hates — more than anything — being asked questions.'

At first Pinguel had tried to catch the owl, but it had always soared expertly away. Lately he had ignored him.

'My father,' Ogren had told him, 'thinks the owl a lunatic, though harmless. After all, where's his family? What pleasure could he get, living all alone? "The owl with the broken brain", father calls him.'

Now Pinguel halted and called out:

'Don't fly away! Isn't the forest cold and empty this evening? How did you become addicted to solitude, owl? Why is it that you hate questions?'

The owl hopped from his branch into a cold shadow, and soared away.

'What is your life *for*, owl?' Pinguel called out in his slightly husky voice, like that of a singer who has spent too much time rehearsing. 'What is your *purpose*?'

He went through the trees, at first following the owl and then hardly knowing where he was going.

So what is *your* purpose, he asked himself.

He had been travelling for hours, through the forest of his own thoughts. Just when the last glow of sunset was replaced by moonlight, his skin touched a thread of fine stuff, not as strong as cotton. Ahead an orange light blinked, and went out abruptly. Then a bell rang for no more than two seconds, like the school's, except shriller.

The forest was still, as though none of these things had happened.

Pinguel advanced cautiously, certain some creature was nearby, watching. Perhaps the owl, and he was near his home. Then he halted and listened to the silence.

Moonlight cast a glow on branches and leaves everywhere except for one place, as wide as a tree trunk, that lay in deepest darkness.

He felt afraid of this pure shadow, yet found himself moving towards it.

He kept going until he made out, above, rippling in a breeze, a canopy made of cloth. It was this that caused the darkness beneath.

He halted. Something or someone lived here, far from blats.

Just as he was about to start forward again, an orange light came on, and a picture sprang before him.

A blat with thin, grey hair falling past his shoulders was sitting on a chair made of wooden slats, holding a glass containing a green drink. The ankle of one leg rested just above the knee of the other. Wearing a faded khaki jumper and trousers, and bright red, woolly slippers, he held out a hand in a welcoming gesture, inviting Pinguel to join him on his verandah. The fingers were thin and bony. The blat was very, very old.

'Join me for an evening drink, won't you? It has been my custom for many years now to sit here and watch the darkness fall over the forest.' He stood up. 'Mint julep? Please, be seated. Back in a moment.'

Beneath the table, Pinguel noticed, was a crossbow with a single silver arrow in the breach. The wire was drawn right back; it was ready to fire.

'Yes,' the old blat acknowledged, returning with two drinks. 'I could have shot you. No doubt you knew that inside any darkness there will always be someone looking out. I saw you halt.' The old blat sipped his drink, and Pinguel followed suit. It tasted of mint and honey.

'Let me introduce myself. My name is Sarin.'

When Pinguel spoke, his voice sounded strangely loud in the dark night:

'I have heard of you. You were a Far Scout. There aren't any Far Scouts any more.'

Sarin nodded. 'Good. I am not entirely forgotten. Nowadays blats prefer television news to a Far Scout.' He turned to Pinguel. His nose curled over a little, giving it a beak-like look. He seemed to be waiting for something. Then Pinguel realised: he hadn't introduced himself.

'My name is Pinguel. I'm Cliffkin the sorcerer's son, Cliffkin de Mandiargues.'

'Yes, I've heard of him.'

'His adopted son, I mean. My mother brought me into the forest.'

'Mmm, I could tell that you weren't a blat, and not only because of your nose. Not a merryn either: legs are too long. You don't try to make yourself invisible, do you? You keep on advancing. Thoroughly unblatlike.'

They were silent for a few seconds, then Sarin spoke softly:

'Have you thought of becoming a Far Scout yourself? Let me tell you something.' He drummed his fingernails against his glass. 'The blats need one, now more than ever. There are no longer many places in the world that have not been explored and settled by knights and dragons, or by the mechanised races. The Deep Forest is one of the last.'

He sighed. 'Far Scouts don't make much money, but that's all right if you don't have a taste for luxury. The pension is enough for five and, if you skimp a bit on food, six mint juleps a day. I suppose you'd better be getting back now, or your father will be worrying.'

FOURTEEN ~~~

Pinguel tried to imagine that he was a Far Scout, exploring a world of loneliness and distance.

'Far scouting?' Cliffkin wondered aloud, when Pinguel had told him of his meeting with Sarin. 'Yes, perhaps that is your fate. But it is hard to conceive of just how far those scouts — for Sarin was the last — used to travel. Imagine the distance from here to the nearest edge of the forest, then multiply that by ten. Have you arrived yet? Have the trees parted, and can you see, ahead, clear distance with nothing to block your view? No, you are still well into the forest. Multiply the distance that you imagined by ten, and you will have some idea. Think what a feat it was for your mother, and for Faringaria and the other refugees, to reach here. Your mother came along the spur, which has its own dangers, quite different to those of the forest. She may have had help, in ways unknown to us. Faringaria and the others? They were forced to use the rivers; some travelled along the banks and took refuge from knights and wolves in the water, others used frail boats. But those in my desk are far from being all who have sought refuge here. No, perhaps they are a hundredth, a thousandth part. They are the ones who survived.'

Especially at night before falling asleep, or in quiet moments during the day, such as at school when the teacher was explaining something that he already knew, Pinguel would think of the edges of the forest, the very border where the trees met the bare lands beyond. He thought of himself in the branches there, looking out, and tried to imagine what he would see. Would it be the faintly foolish, pompous world of pyramids and marching processions that most blats seemed to think it was? Or would it be something darker, something that would cause him to open his eyes wide and to retreat as quickly as he could back into the safety of Deep Forest?

PART FOUR

FIFTEEN ~~~

At the beginning of the Spring Term in every blat's third year of high school, he or she was required to begin three years of part-time (on Wednesday afternoons, three until half-past five) warrior training. These lessons were usually given by retired officers of the Spear Guard, or less often the Arrow Guard, who were allowed to earn a little money in this way without losing full payment of their pension.

At Pinguel's school the lessons were taken by Boboscular Conte d'Arbuisson, an ex-captain of the Spear Guard who in his youth had been slender and handsome, with a fine long nose coming to a sharp point at its tip, and a good arm both for throwing a spear and for driving a golf ball with great accuracy the length of the long fairway on the Evening Course.

Now, aged one hundred and twenty-four, his nose had turned red at its tip (pink elsewhere), his hair was the colour of the wiry tangles used to clean pots, and he walked with a duck-like waddle, leaning back with his feet pointing outwards to support a plump stomach.

The lessons were held on a covered platform that had once been a cotton storage depot. (New cable lines along the 306 and 324 routes had allowed harvesters to take their cotton directly to the warehouses, with no need for such depots.) Between the interwoven twigs of the platform were wisps of ancient, yellow cotton that made the floor even smoother than that of a normal blat platform. On the support posts were rusty iron rings, through which the wires for holding the bales had been strung.

Boboscular stood before a blackboard and hitched up his grey, captain's trousers (with a red stripe down the outside of each leg). His voice had remained that of the dashing young officer he had once been. With its fine clarity, it made Pinguel think of early morning in topmost branches.

'Welcome, students.' He smiled at the sixty-three boys and girls.

Next to Pinguel, Ogren's eyes were sharp with concentration. At last (the boy seemed to be thinking) after years of maths, history and language study, here was something exciting. He had already decided that after school, like his father, he would go straight into the Spear Cadets.

'What does one have to know, to be a blat warrior?' Boboscular asked. Either ignoring or not seeing the many raised hands, he went straight on:

'It's simple. The skill comes in learning, and becoming good at, Running Away, always the most sensible response when one is faced with danger.'

The children were silent. They already knew this, though they couldn't have said exactly how. It was like the rules of golf: they could not remember a time when they hadn't known what it was that blat warriors did.

'After Running Away, we will study Silence and Invisibility. After this comes Deception, followed by Advanced Deception, which will be taken only by those of you who have managed to pass the Invisibility exam. I should warn you, right now, that only a quarter of you will achieve this. True invisibility is difficult to attain, and is an essential prerequisite for Advanced Deception. In these last two courses you will learn how a

blat can trick even the most ferocious warriors —
whether wolf, merryn, human, or knight — into believing
that *they* are the ones in danger.'

Boboscular clapped his hands. 'Enough for one day!
Next week we begin the art of Running Away. I will see
you then.'

On the following Wednesday the student warriors
climbed among the branches and practised what
Boboscular called 'Preparatory Listening'.

'Only when you have remained still and silent for long
enough to be certain where the danger is coming from
can you act. Otherwise it is mere panic, not a proper
retreat. And panic' — Boboscular waggled a plump
forefinger back and forth — 'panic can lead you into the
claws or mouths of the enemy just as easily as it can take
you away from them.'

So they practised listening. 'Hear that?' Boboscular
asked, every time a cable car approached. 'Where exactly
is the noise coming from? Remember, better to remain
still and silent until you know for certain.'

Next week, he promised, they would practise holding
their breath. They would find that this helped greatly
with listening for danger.

Pinguel had climbed to a branch as far as possible
from Ogren. As the class broke up he called out, 'I'll see
you at the course', and when his friend was out of sight
he caught up with Boboscular.

'Captain?'

'Yes?' The huge blat turned, and Pinguel watched
closely for his reaction. He blinked, and opened his
mouth a fraction, showing no more than slight surprise at

being addressed by the non-blat (or half-blat, as some said) whom he had spotted straightaway in his class.

'I wanted to ask a question, sir. I wanted to ask, why should we always run away? Couldn't we *fight*, ever?'

The Captain stood in silence, looking down at Pinguel, who barely came to the middle button of his grey shirt. The boy had time to wonder if he hadn't got himself into trouble by asking such a question.

Slowly, the Captain shook his head.

'That has been suggested, even in my lifetime, even by senior officers. It is not as ridiculous as it may sound at first. The answer is simple. We blats' — he used these two words kindly, to include Pinguel — 'do not have the heart for it. We do not have the necessary coldness to become life-takers, invaders, conquerors, in short to live by forcing others to die. Perhaps as a last, final, and ultimate resort. But such a time has never yet come.' He gestured around him. 'The forest is huge. By the time they are grown up, blats are expert at vanishing into shadows. Our plan is to remain silent, hiding, until any invader has gone. And why should anyone except blats stay for long in the forest? Even if they were to burn our trees, the soil is too rocky for them to grow crops. Invaders may come' — he waved an arm overhead — 'or birds may grow savage from time to time; but we have generally found that it suits us better to retreat and hide until the trees are safe once again. Does that answer your question?'

Pinguel nodded, and in truth could find nothing to say against the Captain's answer. Yet in the back of his mind was a worry, like a feeling of having forgotten something important without being able to remember exactly what.

That afternoon, leaving the old cotton platform, he spotted Sog, the owl, watching him from the highest branches. He was so used to this by now that he merely waved, and didn't give the owl another look as he headed off towards home.

SIXTEEN ~~~

By the middle of winter the warrior classes lost their appeal, even for those who, like Ogren, wished to join the Spear or Arrow Guard.

For as long as two hours at a time the students remained among branches. Snowflakes searched for a way to the forest floor as Boboscular lectured his pupils on the importance of not shivering, and of keeping a hand over the mouth to prevent foggy breath emerging.

One afternoon, Pinguel found himself inching along his branch until he was out of sight of the Captain. He was obeying an impulse, or rather was being overcome by one. He longed to escape from class. Half an hour remained, but he couldn't wait.

He couldn't, that was all.

Suddenly he was sick of all this hiding and sitting still. Why, if anyone ever did invade the forest, he at least would do something about it, would make them suffer for having dared to threaten blats.

He lowered himself to a broader branch, where a snowflake touched his non-blattish nose.

He crept a few paces further, then swung through cold air, heading for the uninhabited (by blats) parts of the forest. Never had he felt so free. He halted, then followed the downward progress of a snowflake that seemed especially determined to reach the forest floor alive.

Why bother? he wondered.

It looped past a leaf, just missing it, and plunged through the very narrowest part of a branch-fork. Yet when it reached the ground it would die anyway. Why care so much about not perishing sooner? Or was there something about the thrill of avoiding obstacles, of exploring depths, that made the journey worthwhile?

Lower down, the snowflake careered into a tree trunk. The boy halted and approached the spot. A patch of wetness against lichen-covered bark was all that remained of the flake.

Pinguel sat on a branch, and had begun to feel cold and to think about going home, when he glimpsed something below.

He watched, perfectly still.

It was a wolf, the brown-grey fur such perfect camouflage against fallen leaves that Pinguel wouldn't have noticed it if, as the wolf made a sharp turn around a tree, he hadn't glimpsed the line of white fur along its underside. So it was a young wolf, possibly a school student like himself.

He found himself following the animal, and going lower.

Perhaps this wolf was the same as him. Had it grown tired of Third Year Hunting and Killing, and slunk off from class? Perhaps the wolf, too, found himself held tight by a desire too strong, for the moment, to defeat.

Pinguel remembered some of Madam's stories of blats and wolves. Had those heroic, wonderful days ever existed, or had life always been much as it was now: a matter of studying hard, keeping things tidy, and getting a good job?

He went ahead of the wolf, and lower. The branches down here were broader than those above. Instead of swinging from tree to tree, travel was more a matter of jumping and keeping balance. Pinguel knew that if he kept this up he would sooner or later stumble over a shard of bark and fall, or at least make enough noise for the wolf to hear. And from only a couple of metres down it would be simple for the wolf to spring up and grab him.

Even now, the young wolf was sniffing the air and pausing with its ginger-tipped ears on alert, as though sensing the bundle of strange emotions above him.

Pinguel, further ahead, waited for the wolf to pass beneath. He sensed rather than knew in words what he was about to do. He trembled as an icy gust blew against his face, and the trees around him became urgent, like a forest of exclamation marks.

The wolf's paws made padding, confident sounds on the dampened leaves and moss that formed the forest floor. When the wolf was directly below, Pinguel jumped. The wolf had a front paw on a root. Just before Pinguel landed, the animal looked up, but hardly had time to growl before the boy (only the height of the wolf's leg from claw-tip to knee) landed on his back just where neck joined body.

The wolf's fur had looked soft from above, but was actually more like wire or the bristles of a brush to the touch. Pinguel clutched it with all his strength and pressed his cheek against the animal's neck, expecting it to career through the forest, to buck and jump, roll him over, snap around to get at his legs, and writhe against trees to scrape him away.

Instead the wolf stood still, front paw on the tree-root, and did nothing.

Then it gave the slightest possible shudder. It had been remaining so still that it had forgotten to breathe. Now it sighed deeply.

It turned its head around and — Pinguel supposed — was able to see his shoe and leg. Then it looked down, and spoke:

'So I have a mad blat on my back. Are you going to stick a poisoned knife into me? Is this the start of a blat attack against wolves? If so, would you please do it now? I'm cold, standing here.'

Pinguel kept his grip, head pressed down. The wolf was far cleverer than he had suspected. It was waiting for him to relax, then it would shake him off and gobble him up. But as soon as he told himself this he began to doubt it.

The wolf sounded faintly tired, and its voice was thoughtful, reminding Pinguel of his father, especially on Thursday nights when he spoke to Faringaria.

'Well?' the wolf asked. 'Are you going to speak? I like this part of the forest because it's so empty. My name is Graf. What's yours?'

'Pinguel,' the boy finally answered, still holding on tight.

'Ah, Pinguel. You must be very frightened. I don't suppose you do have a poisoned dagger, do you? Listen, I'm going to walk over to that tree, the one with the fork quite low and the branches not far above. You can jump off my back and be away in half a second, or you can make yourself invisible, like a true blat. But I won't attack you. Instead, I'd like to talk. So stay within earshot at least. You're brave enough to jump onto a wolf's back. Surely you have the courage to hang around for a bit?'

Pinguel felt the wolf's heartbeat: slow, even thoughtful, like his voice.

'All right,' the boy answered finally. 'Over to the tree.'

Here, Pinguel jumped to the branch, just as the wolf had suggested, but instead of rushing for a higher place he stood quite still, feet planted wide. He felt ready for anything, but the wolf did not attack.

Instead he stared, then relaxed onto his haunches, ears pointed straight up in curiosity.

'Well, well,' Graf began in his civilised voice. 'Look at you. Not a blat, nor a merryn either. That certainly isn't a blat nose. Who are you?'

'I am a blat. At least, I live with blats.'

'I see.' The wolf nodded.

'Why didn't you attack me? Why don't you now?'

The wolf's eyes were the colour of an autumn leaf with the light of late afternoon behind it. Now his ears were pressed back in a kindly way.

'I don't belong to any particular pack,' Graf answered. 'That's because I don't go along with the wolf motto. Have you heard it? "Savagery Above All".' Graf shrugged, and gave his ear a quick scratch with a hind leg. 'Savagery has never much agreed with me. I prefer quieter pleasures, such as painting. I don't even hunt voles or rabbits for food; I prefer peanut butter sandwiches. In fact, I don't eat meat at all. I have my own den not far away. Do you want to see it?'

The forest was silent as Pinguel considered this. Graf continued:

'Follow me through the trees. We don't want any wolves — or blats, I suppose — to see us together.'

So Graf set off and, a little behind at first, but catching up as he climbed to the narrower branches, Pinguel followed. After twelve minutes, which due to the cold silence of this part of the forest felt much longer, Graf came to a crack between a boulder and a tree, where he halted and wagged his tail.

'Please, come inside,' he invited.

Pinguel thought of his mother. Almost certainly, as Cliffkin had told him, she had been killed by wolves. And now one was inviting him into its den, from which there could be no escape.

Then Pinguel remembered the snowflake that he had followed until it had died against the tree trunk.

'Yes, I'll come.' He jumped from the branch to the tree root, then to the ground.

He was standing on the earth, as he had never done before.

It felt weird. It had no *give* in it. Even a sturdy branch would sink fractionally beneath the weight of the lightest blat. And the whole forest was always shivering, shifting, or swaying to breezes and winds. But this earth felt dead, it was so still.

'My,' murmured Graf, 'you are a brave blat, if you are a blat. Come inside. We shouldn't be seen together, should we?'

The den was dark, and smelt of earth and something like mushrooms. Before Pinguel's eyes could adjust, Graf, sitting back and using his front paws just like hands, struck a match and lit a lamp on a table made of rough boards.

Two walls of the den were made of rock, the other two of tree-root polished to a deep red; all four were nearly covered with squares of colour framed in plain wood. As Pinguel stepped closer, he saw that these were paintings. One showed a whole family of wolves seated at a table, holding knives and forks, obviously having dinner, a normal sort of scene except that the table was on a fluffy cloud like those that simply drift across a blue sky, meaning no harm to anyone, and this cloud (and therefore the wolf family and their table as well) was floating far above the forest.

The next showed a wolf in a blue gown, seated in a comfortable chair with his legs on a windowsill and a book open on his lap. Beyond the window was an evening sky, one or two stars among the purple, and a single red cloud from which a small dragon was emerging.

Most of the paintings were of wolves in various fantastic situations (lying in a bed that was floating down a river towards a waterfall, playing cards and drinking something from a cup while falling from a cliff ...) but some were of more ordinary subjects: a bowl of fruit on a tablecloth, flowers in a vase, and so on.

From a cupboard at the far end of the room Graf had taken a bottle containing a purple liquid and two glasses.

'Please, sit down. No, the chair's a bit low for you. Better sit on the table, here. I'll get you a cushion. There. Like some wortleberry juice?'

He laughed, but in a way that didn't seem at all relaxed. It was short, almost a bark, and he cut it off abruptly.

'Well, what do you think?' There was a tremor in his voice, and his bristly eyebrows had come down over his eyes, shadowing them with self-doubt. 'Do you like my paintings?' He took a long drink.

Pinguel spoke the truth:

'They're wonderful. Great paintings. You're an artist!'

Graf's gloomy frown returned. 'You aren't just saying that, to be friendly? You really mean it?'

'Yes, I do. I like your paintings very much.'

Graf peered carefully at Pinguel, then sighed.

'I'm sorry. It isn't fair of me to interrogate you this way. But you can imagine what it's like for a wolf, being a painter. All the wolves I know have no time for art. Some pretend to take an interest because they want to be thought refined; but beyond that, nothing. All they really care about is fighting and hunting.' Graf sat forward. 'But I'm being too self-absorbed, as usual. What about you? What in the forest's name possessed you to jump onto my back? Or did you fall, perhaps?'

Pinguel looked down into his glass of purple liquid. He felt a strong urge to trust this wolf.

'I'm not sure. It was an impulse. Maybe I wanted a fight. I'm stronger than I look, older too, or that's what my father tells me. My adoptive father, I should say. My natural father died before I was born. As for my mother' — here Pinguel looked straight at Graf — 'she was killed by wolves.'

The den was silent. 'I see.' Graf bowed his head, and spoke softly. 'I don't want to make excuses, but I think that you should bear in mind the sort of animal most of us are. To the majority of wolves, blats are no more than a rare source of food, one that occasionally falls, like a gift, from trees. But you aren't a blat, are you? What are you?'

'I don't know. I'll find out one day, I suppose.'

Absent-mindedly, Graf reached for a sheet of paper and a scrap of charcoal, and began to sketch Pinguel.

'I'm sure you will,' he said. 'In the meantime . . .'

He was interrupted by a knock at the door. A voice called out:

'Graf! Main Den, quick. General Order, from the Council. Hurry!'

The door started to open. Pinguel stood up, but Graf came quickly towards him. 'In there, into the cupboard,' he whispered. 'Hide. I'll be back. Have no idea what this could be. Some emergency or other.'

'Come, Graf,' came the voice, louder now, and definitely that of a wolf. 'What's going on? Who have you got in there? Smells strange. Found a girlfriend at last?'

'No, no, brother. Coming.' Graf snatched his half-finished sketch of Pinguel from the table, shoved it into the cupboard after the boy, and pushed the door shut.

In complete darkness, Pinguel smelt cheese and wortleberry juice. Then he heard Graf say, 'Coming! Yes, here I am. So what's the great hurry?' and the door slammed shut.

Pinguel stepped out of the cupboard. Graf had left the lanterns on.

I have to be getting home, the boy told himself. Cliffkin will be worried.

Then he heard a gurgling near the door.

It still felt strange to be on firm ground, let alone in a wolf's den.

He trod on something wet that definitely hadn't been here before. He jumped back, behind a leg of the table. Was this some sort of trap?

Water lapped at his feet.

Not knowing what to think, he splashed his way to the door, high for someone his size, and pushed it a little way open. Water rushed through the gap over his shoes.

He stepped into a knee-deep flood that — as Pinguel stood there, too shocked for the moment to move — was rapidly getting deeper. Like river rapids, it surged over tree-roots and frothed into hollows. A scum of moss fragments, dirt and leaves made it appear as if the ground was a carpet being dragged away.

Pinguel climbed onto the roof of Graf's den in time to see a party of wolves sprint past. Now waist-high to Pinguel, the water had not yet reached a quarter of the way up the wolves' legs. As the boy climbed higher, snowflakes swirled around him.

He had expected it to be raining, but there was only snow. So where was the water coming from? He climbed higher, travelling towards home, and only when he was almost there did he notice, over one side of the sky (the other was black, though strangely empty of stars) a glow that started off red and, coming closer to the horizon, passed through shades of orange down to a bright, flickering yellow.

It looked like fire. But that was the direction of the Cold Mountains, and how could *they* possibly be on fire, made as they were of ice?

He stood on an upper branch with snowflakes sticking to his hair, and the sky glowed red, orange and yellow.

He hurried home.

SEVENTEEN

Blats were crowded onto branches, verandahs and platforms, watching the strangely-coloured sky and eagerly talking. Cliffkin was on his verandah with Ogren, Strolgo, Madam and Clerkwellstone. They greeted Pinguel with relief.

'We thought something might have happened to you,' Cliffkin explained.

'No, I'm all right. But what is happening to the sky?'

'None of us knows,' the sorcerer answered, moving closer to the verandah railing.

'And the ground?' Pinguel wondered. 'Have you seen it? Deep with water, flowing from over there.'

Strolgo was wearing his metal helmet and carrying a steel-tipped spear, which meant that he was on duty and prepared for anything. In keeping with this, he was entirely serious.

'Yes, we have seen the water,' he stated.

'Nothing like this has ever been recorded, either in the Annals or the Legends,' murmured Madam, voice full of wonder.

From behind him, Pinguel noticed a murmuring. It was Clerkwellstone:

'Cause and effect, effect and cause.'

But the old repairer often muttered to himself, and blats had got into the habit of paying no attention until he spoke out, intending to be heard.

Young Giles d'Ofray, the baker's apprentice, climbed from below and shouted to the party on his father's verandah (though by the proud tone of his voice it was obvious that he was conscious of being heard by everyone all around):

'Now the water's over sixty paces high!'

Clerkwellstone stepped forward, the warm light from the sky giving his skin a bronzed look.

'Cause and effect!' he proclaimed. 'It's the heart of winter, so water should be frozen into ice. As it is flowing, ice must have melted. Cause?' He pointed at the sky. 'A fire on the other side of the Cold Mountains, one large enough to melt the deep winter ice and send it flowing here. Cause and effect!'

Cliffkin immediately remembered what Sog, the owl, had told him. At the time it had sounded like a story, something made up, now the memory made him shiver.

'On the other side of those uncrossable mountains,' he murmured to himself as much as to anyone else, 'lies a Great Forest, like ours, and in the trees live blats, like us.'

Madam took her old friend's arm. 'It's written in the Annals, Cliffkin: second chapter, sixth verse. "And the lands," she quoted from memory, "shall be divided by mountains of ice into three parts. There will be a Great Forest, a Deep Forest, and an Ocean. And the only one to traverse the ice shall do so in days when there are worlds to discover, and dangers grow like leaves in a spring forest."'

Strolgo gave a tolerant smile, which Ogren, looking up at his father (whom he took to be not only the strongest but also the wisest person in the world), imitated. He glanced across at his friend, Pinguel, to see if he too were smiling at Madam's solemn nonsense from the dusty old Annals.

But no, Pinguel wasn't smiling.

And one shall cross ... These words rang in his mind, and he imagined himself, Pinguel, at the base of the Cold Mountains, all that ice at his face.

Blats from the lower platforms shifted themselves and their possessions to the upper platforms and apartments of relatives and friends. Pinguel saw Miss Bardle two verandahs away, giving instructions to a strong nephew who had a rolled-up carpet balanced on his shoulder.

The glow in the sky deepened. While the night advanced, and a damp chill entered the air, the yellow turned orange, and the red purple. The water rose to a depth of two hundred and twenty paces, just high enough to threaten the lowest golfing platforms, then began to fall.

None of the blats in the forest went to bed before two o'clock in the morning, and the next day was declared a public holiday to allow various committees to discuss what had happened.

Pinguel wondered whether to tell his father about Graf, but decided, for now, to keep his new friendship to himself.

EIGHTEEN ~~~

Pinguel woke at first light, while Cliffkin was still asleep, and went outside.

The sky was the grey of worn bark; the air smelt of smoke. Leaves, moss, sludge and dirty bubbles covered the forest floor. He went lower, and noticed a paler streak.

It was the white fur of a wolf's belly. Sprawled out, the body looked headless. Pinguel climbed closer, careful to stay out of wolf-reach.

How many wolves had died? Were there any left, in Deep Forest? Before last night, Pinguel, like a good blat, might have rejoiced to have the forest free of wolves.

Now he raced through the trees.

On the roof of his den, Graf was holding a painting between his front paws. He sniffed.

'Pinguel, is that you? I warn you, it isn't safe here. All the packs are out, looking for their dead. There's a funeral tonight, in the Main Clearing.' Graf sighed.

Around him were other paintings and scraps of rag. He was drying their surfaces. Beneath more rags lay a heap of muddy frames.

'Luckily, I paint in oils: waterproof. Still, I'll have to re-stretch and frame the canvases, and there'll be cracks to restore.'

Pinguel sat on a low branch, legs dangling. 'But you're alive,' he found himself saying, as though this piece of good fortune might take the wolf's mind off the damage to his paintings. 'I hope your friends and family are all right.'

Graf put down the painting. 'I don't have friends, except for you. Family? All safe. Most of us reached the main den in time and barricaded the door. It's near the river, which rises occasionally, though never as high as last night, so there's a system of watertight doors. We had leaks in the roof, and a few anxious moments, but we were all right. It was the long-distance hunters who didn't make it.' He gave a tired smile, and Pinguel realised that his new friend probably hadn't slept all night. 'But here you are,' Graf shook his head, 'a blat or near-blat, concerned about wolves. I'd ask you inside but it's a dreadful mess.'

'No, no. I'll visit you again soon.' Pinguel had stood up and was about to go.

'No! Wait, you don't know what caused the flood, do you? Our scientists think it was the river, and the destruction of something they call a dam far beyond the forest.'

The wolves, Pinguel realised, could know nothing about the fire beyond the Cold Mountains. How could they, confined to the ground, rarely even seeing the sky? Pinguel explained Clerkwellstone's theory, and left the wolf murmuring to himself:

'A fire beyond mountains made of ice. Melting mountains of ice. Now how would you paint that? Blue, orange, red . . .'

As Pinguel travelled through the forest he noticed a fluttering above, as the owl, Sog, flew away from watching him talk with Graf.

NINETEEN ~~~

The sky kept its ashen colour for three days, then a strong wind scoured it back to blue. A chill from the unnaturally wet forest floor caused those older blats who suffered from rheumatism to complain of a more intense aching in their joints than ever. Blats wore their heaviest jackets for weeks longer than normal, until the middle of spring, then came two weeks of warm days and apricot skies that returned the forest to how it had been before the flood. The moss regrew over earth and rocks, and the dried mud peeled from tree trunks. Graf restored his paintings, cleaned out his den, and began a portrait of Pinguel.

'If any wolf sees it,' he told the boy, 'I'll tell them it's entirely from imagination.'

The wolf and boy became best friends. Graf was twenty-two, young for a wolf of the Deep Forest, where wolves lived to one hundred and eighty (in rare cases to two hundred and ten). The only thing about him that irritated Pinguel was a tendency to hopeless sadness. When it was getting dark, and Pinguel was about to leave, the wolf tended to fall into gloom.

'If only I were a blat,' he would sigh. 'If only I could live with a crowd of others, interested in painting. I imagine a huge dining table instead of this little one here, and every evening when I'd finished painting I'd sit at it and talk with friends. With blats' — he gave an extra heavy sigh — 'who cared about me, and about my work. Anyway, yes, I know I'm sulking. Forgive me. I'm tired. Have you noticed how this sort of sadness comes most often when one is tired?'

In trying to cheer his friend up, Pinguel would often find himself saying the wrong thing:

'I don't think tiredness is the reason,' he would suggest. 'Perhaps your trouble is that you have too good an imagination. You picture a perfect world, and when you compare it with the real one, it makes you sad. So —'

'No, no.' The wolf would hold up both his paint-splattered paws. 'Don't ask me to make myself content with things as they are. Please, I couldn't bear it.'

TWENTY ~~~

Pinguel's favourite time for visiting Graf was on Wednesdays, following warrior training. He no longer went home with Ogren. The two friends had grown apart over their years of junior high school.

Once, after meeting Graf, Pinguel had spoken to Ogren in a thoughtful way, as though to himself:

'You know, all this talk of the savagery of wolves. I wonder what would happen if we tried to make friends with them?'

Ogren's eyes had widened, and although his mouth opened, he said nothing in his astonishment. It was Pinguel who broke the silence by giving a laugh that implied he had been joking.

'Ha! Ha!' Ogren joined in. 'You say such funny things, little Pinguel.'

One summer afternoon, following warrior training, Pinguel saw Ogren leave the old, ex-cotton platform with some of his friends. They were talking about the World Human Golf Championships, to be televised next week. Seeing his old friend go without even looking in his, Pinguel's, direction, the boy felt as sad as when he had, years ago, swung through the trees for the first time with Cliffkin on his way to school. Things had changed. Maybe something had been gained, but something had been lost too.

The World Human Golf Championships had always been of interest to some blats, mainly because it showed them how inferior this foreign game was to their own. Human courses contained no upwhisks or downslides, and each shot had only one possible target. Worse, everything was on a single level, and there was sunlight everywhere. How could anyone concentrate in such glare?

But interest in human golf had spread among blats with the appearance of Hugo, a boy only twelve years old, who had so far beaten enough eminent adult golfers to qualify for the World Championships. Hugo's appearance and background fascinated blats (as it did many humans). In babyhood he had suffered from a disease that had left him bent over, with a humped back and drooping eye. Before becoming a golfing star he had been an outcast among his fellow schoolchildren. Now the boy lived on an ocean liner called the *Orestea*, with his parents.

'Look at that club,' pointed out Strolgo to his son, when the World Championship match was about to start. The TV showed Hugo taking a practice swing.

Many of Madam's friends and relations were crowded into her lounge room to watch the television (the same set that Pinguel, so many years ago, had tried to stab from underneath with a pencil). Taller adults had been made to sit at the back to allow others to see.

'A blat club,' repeated Ogren dutifully, as he reached for the potato crisps.

Blats had been noticing this for ages. As with their own clubs, the handle and heads of Hugo's were made of gold (or brass, it was impossible to tell on the TV screen) and the stick of polished, dark wood.

The match started. Spectators cheered from their pyramid-shaped grandstands, above each of which was a billboard proclaiming, 'Long Live the Grand Duke Pinchie du Henderson'.

Hugo's main rival was a young man with yellow, curling hair known as Frederick the Great. He stood tall and proud, and hit his first shot straight onto the green.

Hugo came next. He looked small and forlorn with his bent-over back, clothes too big for him, shirtsleeves hanging over fingers, and trousers bunched up on shoes. He closed his eyes and hit the ball into the middle of a small forest.

'Hugo always starts badly,' murmured Madam.

The boy's next shot went into a pond, Frederick's into the hole.

The tournament went on like this until Hugo seemed to have no chance of winning. The humans in the pyramid stands were silent, as were the blats gathered around their TV screens in Deep Forest. 'We had expected a better contest than this,' complained a TV commentator.

Pinguel watched closely. Hugo trailed his club behind him as he walked from pond to forest, from forest to pond. Unlike Frederick, he had only one club, and therefore no caddy to help him.

Then Hugo stopped. On the horizon was a grey cloud. He turned away from the camera, but another one on top of a grandstand picked him up in its zoom lens.

'Ah, we've seen this before, haven't we Ron?' the commentator asked his partner.

'Yes, Pete, at Gala Springs on the thirteenth hole.'

The crowd remained hushed.

Hugo reached into his baggy shirt pocket.

'Not all viewers will have seen this,' Ron hurried to explain, 'because the Gala Springs match wasn't televised internationally, but ... There it is! The lucky doll. It's said that it has been in the boy's family since — Look!'

The blats had heard of the doll, but had never seen it. They sat forward, fascinated, as wisps of steam rose from the ventilation grille at the back of the set.

Hugo reached into his back pocket and ... Imagine the watching blats' surprise when he brought out a tin-helmeted figure, wearing a green shirt, brown waistcoat and trousers, and holding a long spear ...

'A member of the Spear Guard,' gasped Strolgo, squeezing his son's hand.

'A blat,' confirmed Madam.

'It can't be,' Cliffkin whispered.

'No,' put in Clerkwellstone. 'A doll. Isn't moving. Isn't alive.'

Hugo raised the doll — or blat — to his face, whispered something, then moved it to his ear.

'It's speaking to him,' Ogren insisted, looking at Pinguel for confirmation.

But Pinguel only stared.

The commentators speculated:

'Apparently, Ron, the figure, or doll, is a sort of lucky charm. Gives Hugo confidence. Reminds him of his old coach or something.'

'He certainly needs confidence now, Pete.'

The sky over the golf course had darkened.

'Looks ominous,' said Ron, 'but remember, viewers, these matches are *never* cancelled due to rain.'

Like a sudden growth of fungus, umbrellas shot up over the spectators. Hugo put the blat-like figure back into his pocket and, before hitting his next shot, tightly closed his eyes. Lightning forked through the sky. He swung his club, and the ball soared and bounced only once before landing straight in the hole.

Everyone — blats and humans — cheered. (Everyone except for Frederick the Great, who, as he swung to hit his next shot, slipped on the now soaking grass and sent his ball scudding only a couple of feet.)

Hugo continued to play brilliantly in the soggy

conditions, while Frederick played worse and worse, until on the last green the scores were level. Every so often the commentators mentioned just how many millions of dollars the winner would receive as prize money. Ron in particular was enraptured by the thought of this:

'Frederick is already a rich man,' he acknowledged, 'but Hugo is said to be short of cash, living as he does on a luxury ocean liner.'

'Sure, it must be expensive to run a ship like that,' agreed Pete.

And now the rain was pouring down. The golfers would have to hit their balls over several broad puddles to get near the hole.

'I don't think we'll be seeing any fancy shots here,' said Pete.

'*Imagine* what it would be like,' Ron mused, 'living on your own ocean liner. All that space. Your own swimming pool. Just think, you could travel around the world so that it would always be summer, or spring, or whatever season you wanted.'

(Suddenly Madam's room shuddered, and bristled with the noise of snapping twigs. Only Clerkwellstone glanced away from the TV; everyone else remained too absorbed in the match to notice.

'A branch breaking?' he murmured.

The forest was ancient; branches sometimes fell without warning. They would see to it later.)

Hugo again brought out his doll, or whatever it was, and held it out as though showing it the puddle-covered green. You could only tell where the hole was by the white flagpole sticking up from a sheet of water. Then, shielding it from the rain with one hand, he raised the doll to his ear.

'It's telling him something,' Madam whispered.

'You'd have your own cinema, your own tennis court...' Ron continued to muse, caught by the idea of life on board an ocean liner. 'But the sweetest thing would be waking up each morning to an entirely different view.'

Frederick swung, sending up a spray of water. The ball itself soared and fell close to the pole. Perhaps it had rolled *into* the hole.

No one knew until an official in a yellow raincoat came with a glass-bottomed box, saved up for days such as this, and pressed it to the water, which made little slapping and sucking sounds (picked up by all the TV microphones).

'Careful!' Frederick yelled, as a scowl disfigured his handsome face. 'Don't move my ball!'

Cameras peered into the box.

And there was Frederick's ball, right beside the hole.

The champion wiped a string of drops from the brim of his hat and grinned. The tournament was over, this smile said, and he had won.

Meanwhile, Hugo had his eyes closed and seemed to be facing in the wrong direction. Everyone in Madam's room called out to him — *Hugo! Hugo! Look! Turn around!* — when he raised his blat-style gold and wood club, and swung.

The ball went straight up. It soared. The camera drew back to show both Hugo and the ball. Pinguel sat sharply forward. What was that? He had seen something strange, utterly strange. But he didn't mention what it was.

He kept silent and no one else — no one in the whole world, perhaps — noticed it.

The ball soared, the crowd gasped; umbrellas tilted up, allowing rain onto faces and binocular lenses as spectators gaped.

'Being able to cruise foreign shores, and visit cities you'd never seen before,' mused Ron.

'Perhaps the final shot of the most dramatic world championship ever!' gasped Pete.

The ball began to fall. Down, down, landing with a dignified little splash right beside the pole.

An official brought out the glass-bottomed box.

'There we are!' sighed Pete as the screen filled with a picture of grass underwater, looking mournful and quiet as it dreamt of sunnier days, when birds would hop around, crickets would buzz their tunes, and no lawn-mower was approaching. But no sign of the ball.

'And during storms,' Ron continued to dream. 'Imagine then ... The sea tossing, and you snug —'

'Yes, yes,' snapped Pete, 'but where *is* the ball?'

Frederick's face was already twisting into the rich grin of a winner, while Hugo had his hands folded behind his back and was gazing pensively at the water that covered his shoes.

Then the glass-bottomed box moved over the hole. What was that, down there? A flash of white?

'And every evening, as the sun sets —' began Ron.

'Could that be the *ball?*' shouted Pete.

The hand of an important golfing official, the hairs on its back waving in the puddly currents, came into view. Like an eel into its burrow, it snaked into the hole. And came up with ...

Hugo's ball.

Wild cheering — all around the world. Hugo was everyone's favourite, the boy who had been so unpopular at school, who had been poor and lonely, and who was now one of the richest people in the world.

'And sailing over those underwater chasms where the sea is kilometres deep, and merfolk are rumoured to live . . .' speculated Ron.

As blats turned off their TV sets and strolled onto their verandahs, and stretched and sighed, half sad that such an exciting evening's entertainment was over, but also happy that their favourite had won, Clerkwellstone looked up and said:

'That dark patch. What is it?'

Pinguel was about to rush home, to get clear in his mind exactly what he had noticed before Hugo had hit his final shot, but he paused to stand on the verandah railings and peer up. A branch hung down, broken, in front of a shadow over the evening sky.

'I'll see,' cried Pinguel, and he and Ogren at once began to climb, racing each other.

Pinguel was the first to make out feathers, brown and white in the light cast from below. Not an ordinary wing, no, but a long, long one, and fully stretched out. As he climbed along it, and closer, Ogren cried out:

'A bird, a dead bird!'

'Be careful!' called out Madam. 'It may only be hurt.'

But the bird was most certainly dead. Pinguel came upon the shaft of a metal arrow sticking from its side. A great eagle, eyes open dully, and resting upon branches that it had once surveyed from as high as the clouds.

'Shot?' scowled Strolgo, who had climbed up himself once he realised that it was something serious.

Tomorrow, members of the Spear and Arrow Guard would cut free the corpse and bury it down an old mineshaft, but tonight the dead eagle, killed by something or someone unknown, was like an accusing finger pointed at the blats.

'There is much about the world that you do not know,' it warned.

Pinguel caught his father's eye and was surprised to see there (for the first time in the boy's life) a touch of fear.

After Cliffkin had gone to bed, Pinguel thought deeply about the golf match. He seemed to remember clearly that the so-called doll (that so much resembled a member of the blat Spear Guard) had turned its head to look up the fairway. Pinguel replayed this scene in his mind, again and again, but couldn't be absolutely certain.

TWENTY-ONE ~~~

The next morning patrols found eighteen hawks, fifteen falcons, and twelve eagles in the treetops, all shot through with arrows made of light metal. A hawk was still alive. As the warriors of the Spear Guard approached, spears at the ready, the bird blinked, but its golden eyes were placid, with no trace of their old ferocity.

'I am still breathing,' he murmured, then died.

It took five days for parties of soldiers and workers to bury them. Many theories circulated among the blats. The spears were made of aluminium, with the blunt end showing marks of burning. They looked to have been fired from a gun. A war between birds and humans became the accepted explanation, but Cliffkin shook his head when he heard this.

'Shot at such long range ... And surely the birds would never be foolish enough to fight the humans, especially ones armed with arrows such as these.'

The wolves, Pinguel discovered from talking to Graf, knew nothing about it.

'Birds lying among treetops, pierced by arrows,' murmured the artist, already doing a preparatory sketch in his mind. 'It is rare for us even to see a bird. Some of our philosophers claim that the sky doesn't really exist, and say that the trees go up forever, with stranger and stranger creatures making their homes among the branches.'

TWENTY-TWO ~~~

On the second night after the birds, Pinguel was woken by a scratching at his window. He felt a shiver down his back as he reached for the lamp beside his bed.

'No no!' he heard a voice that he had never heard before. 'Do not turn on the light. Do not wake your father. Open the window. It's me, Sog, the owl.'

The bird's two large eyes were staring at Cliffkin, asleep across the room.

'Yes, yes ...' nodded the owl, leaning inside. 'I knew your mother, boy. I haven't always lived alone, among books. I've been away, and have just returned. Weeds have sprouted among my potato plants, and will eventually destroy them. I'll let them. I don't care. Weeds have their allotted time, like all of us. Listen to me.'

Cliffkin turned over in his sleep.

'Your time has come,' the owl whispered, moving his feathery face closer and narrowing his eyes. 'Hear me, young Pinguel. The world is about to end, and you are needed. You are a *titan*. Do you hear that? It won't mean anything to you now, but it will one day. You must come with me, on a journey. The blats should leave too, but they won't be persuaded. They have too much faith in their powers of disappearing and running away. You have time to say goodbye to your father. I will meet you in two hours on the warrior training platform. The first light will just have entered the sky. Bring almost nothing. We shall have to travel quickly.'

Pinguel's first thought when the owl had gone was: 'I'm not going, and that's that.' His second was: 'Why *should* I go? It's ridiculous.'

He remembered the dead birds in the trees, Sarin the Far Scout, the pyramids and marching armies on TV. But if the blats were in danger, shouldn't he stay and help?

He touched his father's shoulder. The old blat sat up, brushing strands of grey hair from his face.

'What? Is something wrong?'

'The owl came, father. Just now.'

'The owl? Sogfort?'

Pinguel nodded, and gave a short laugh of disbelief.

'He said I must go with him, immediately, on a journey for the sake of the blats. He said there was danger, that you should all leave the forest but that you wouldn't because of your — our — faith in disappearing and running away. He said that I was a titan, and would understand later what that meant.'

Cliffkin sat still. 'Yes, well . . .'

He slapped his hands on his knees and took a deep breath.

'We must hurry. You'll need a backpack of provisions, something to hold water, and' — he raised his eyes to the top of the bookshelf — 'there is something else I must give you.'

Pinguel didn't move. 'I must *go*? Just like that? Because an owl came and told me to?'

Cliffkin nodded with complete seriousness. 'Yes, Pinguel, because an owl came. You must leave. And you know it, too.'

The sorcerer turned on the light, dragged a chair over to the bookcase, and got down the Ant Bell.

'And you must take this, and wear it around your neck. And remember, if ever you are in danger, and there seems to be no hope . . . Pinguel, are you listening to me? Please, don't interrupt. If ever you are in great danger you must pull out the wire that is soldered inside, and you must ring this bell.'

'No, you keep it, and if you are in danger —'

But the old sorcerer was shaking his head. 'Hear me, Pinguel. Before you came, I had my work. I had the friendship of Madam. You brought me *happiness*. You're my son. If anything were to happen to you . . . So be quiet. Take the bell. Look after yourself, for my sake, and for the sake of the blats. Now go, please.'

The old sorcerer had a handkerchief out and was blowing his nose while straightening — an odd time to be doing this — his blankets.

So Pinguel stood for a while, too confused to think, then hugged his father, fastened the tiny bell around his neck, and when he had dressed and put on a light backpack containing a change of clothes, toothbrush, blanket, some dried fruit, bread, and a bottle with a screw-top for holding water, he somehow found himself on the verandah and Cliffkin was in the doorway saying:

'I'll say goodbye to Madam, and to Faringaria and the others for you. If things become dangerous, I'll hide them in the cellar, in the earth. And whatever happens, please believe one thing: before too long we'll be back together. Believe that!'

Pinguel climbed into the tree, and it was some minutes before he noticed that he was going in the opposite direction to the warrior training platform. He was heading towards Graf, he realised. He had to say goodbye to his friend.

Despite all the times he had visited the wolf, the ground still sent shivers up the legs of the tree-accustomed boy. He knocked at the door, then heard a groan and someone moving around. He looked over his shoulder. The forest was dark, and he sensed wolves everywhere.

As the door opened, Graf whispered (he already knew who it was, from smelling), '*You*. What's wrong?'

Pinguel stepped quickly inside as Graf lit his lamp.

'You're all . . .' Graf stared at his friend, who had on his best climbing boots, made of rubber and canvas, a warm jacket knitted by Madam, green trousers, and the backpack.

'Yes, Graf. I'm going. I have to leave the forest. An owl told me.'

'*Leave*? Because an owl told you?'

'I've come to say goodbye, my friend. We'll meet again, but —'

'No.' Graf was shaking his head. 'You can't leave. It has taken me this long to find a friend, and now to lose you . . .'

Pinguel held the wolf's front paw, and was about to say goodbye again, when Graf burst out:

'I'll come! You go through the trees; I'll keep track of you from the ground. Here —' He dashed behind his table, pulled out a bag with a strap that went around his neck, and pushed in a few sketchpads, charcoal, three bread rolls, and a jar of peanut butter.

'Don't say anything,' he cautioned as he did this. 'If we get to the end of the forest, if there is such a thing as an end to the forest, then we might all be on the ground together — I assume the owl is coming? — Well, I can give you a ride on my back. That's how we met, remember? Come, I'm ready. Don't slow down for me. I know your scent well enough to follow you, no matter how high in the trees you go.'

Pinguel tried to think whether this was wise, but couldn't. His feeling of relief at having Graf come with him was too great. His only worry was this: 'But if something happens to you?'

'No, no.' The wolf's ears were pointed sharply with eagerness. 'Anyway, what could be worse than to lose my only friend?'

So Pinguel set off through the trees, conscious (although he couldn't see him) of Graf far below, following.

Near the warrior training platform, Pinguel touched the Ant Bell hanging around his neck, and almost fell beneath the weight of all that he was leaving.

'You'll come back,' he told himself. 'You'll live with the blats again. Everything will one day be as it used to be.'

TWENTY-THREE ~~~

'Here I am,' came the soft voice of the owl.

Pinguel told him about Graf (waiting on the ground directly beneath the platform, nose twitching sensitively) and the owl nodded.

'After the forest he may prove a useful ally. But it will be dangerous for him.'

'I told him that.'

The owl was carrying a hessian sack knotted at the top with a length of potato vine. He hoisted this onto his back, and promptly had to sit down beneath the weight.

'I'm not as strong as I used to be. Do you mind if we put a couple of these' — he had opened the top and was taking out round, washed potatoes — 'in your pack? Just a few? Food isn't easy to come by, in the forest. For water, I have a couple of flasks to fill at streams and rivers, and the hollows of trees after rain.'

He blinked his huge eyes at Pinguel. 'But do *you*?'

'Do I what?'

'The wolf knows the journey will be dangerous, but do you?'

'Yes, I do.'

The owl shook his head. The grey light of dawn was touching the edges of leaves.

'No you don't. But I do, because I have a good memory. For you, everything from now on is strange. Good, we begin.'

And so Pinguel left the colony of blats in the heart of Deep Forest, and, as he travelled, his thoughts of the past, and speculations about the future, made the present seem as though it hardly existed, like the space between two books pressed tightly together on a shelf.

PART FIVE

TWENTY-FOUR

Exhausted, hands and feet aching, Pinguel climbed down to see if Graf was still with them. It was evening, and he had never done so much travelling in one day. The wolf was sitting against a trunk, licking a paw. Here the forest was strange: it seemed frozen in silence. The wind in the treetops was the only sound, and it whispered of desolation and loneliness. The only smells were those of bark and leaves. Then Pinguel realised what it was: there were no blats in this part of the forest, none at all.

'I'm not used to this.' Graf gave a brave smile. His bag was on the ground beside him, a piece of charcoal and sketchpad out. 'But you must go back up now. There are wolves around.'

'What about you?' the boy whispered, climbing one branch higher. 'How will you get on with these strange wolves?'

Graf nodded at the paper and charcoal. 'I'll sketch their portraits. I'll tell them I'm a travelling artist — which is true, you know. Wolves may not be fond of artists, but they do appreciate having likenesses of their friends and relations to hang in their dens.'

Sogfort and Pinguel ate raw potatoes for dinner, in the high fork of a tree. They tasted gently hot, and made a crackling sound when bitten. Although too tired for much conversation, Pinguel did ask:

'You said I was a *titan*. What's that? Do I have relatives? Is there a land, somewhere, full of people like me?'

'So I've heard, but I have never seen it,' Sog answered, ruffling his feathers as though this question was the equivalent of a cold breeze. 'I remember hearing that titans are rare. But I am no expert on such matters.'

'You said that you knew my mother.'

The forest was silent, waiting for the owl's response.

'I knew her.' Sogfort had stopped eating. His beak was pale yellow, with a fleck of potato at the tip. 'Your mother was an exceptional woman. Braver than anyone I have known.'

'And my father?' Pinguel asked.

'Your father is a blat sorcerer, called Cliffkin.'

The boy nodded. 'But my real father, my natural father?'

'I did not know your father.'

'Is he alive, somewhere?'

'No, most certainly not. There can be no doubt about that.'

'How do you know?'

The owl brought out his tongue in a flashing movement, and whisked the fleck of potato from his beak.

'I know. I'm a scholar. It's my business to know things. Now we must sleep. The sky is dark. If we stay up all night talking, we will not have the strength for tomorrow.'

TWENTY-FIVE ~~~

The next morning, Pinguel was nearly too sore to move. He groaned as he folded up his blanket and tried to straighten his back. The owl gave a hoot of sympathy.

'My wings, too, are stiff. We will feel better after half an hour of travel.'

That afternoon the forest began to change. A sooty blackness crept over the trees. If anything, the forest now looked even older than where the blats lived. An hour or two before they were due to stop for the night they heard barking, then the cry of a wolf:

'Pinguel, come! See this!'

There was urgency in the voice, but no fear. Pinguel descended the blackened trunk, going from unknown bark-hold to bark-hold, and at its base was Graf sitting with paper and charcoal, sketching frantically. It took Pinguel's eyes a few long seconds to sort out the deep shadowiness here, then he made out what looked like the head of a giant, except constructed of rusting metal, then a leg and arm. As he started back — was the monster asleep, about to awaken? — Graf said, 'See? A knight, dead a long time. Inside the armour is a skeleton. He can't hurt you, not any more. And beneath those leaves, all rotted away except for the bones, is his horse. I wonder what killed them. Oh, hello. You must be Sogfort.'

The owl nodded as he folded up his wings. 'And you are Graf.' He gazed at the remains of the knight.

'Became lost, in search of fugitives,' the owl decided. 'Died from hunger. See his sword over there, propped against the tree, point to the ground? That is his grave-marker. He put it there himself when he was too weak to move further.'

'Lost?' wondered Pinguel. 'But aren't we near the edge of the forest? Don't knights carry compasses?'

Sogfort answered into the leafy gloom:

'They do, but that does not prevent them from going too far in their questing enthusiasm. And as for being near the edge of the forest ... No, we are not nearly there. We have many more days of hard travel ahead of us before we near the fringe.'

Even the leaves hushed themselves as boy and wolf adjusted their thoughts about Deep Forest, and began to understand how truly deep it was.

TWENTY-SIX ～～

On the fifth day of their journey the tree bark changed from black to a carefree shade of brown, and birds (mainly brown finches) began to appear. Pinguel hadn't noticed their absence, although he had felt the silence of the forest as a sort of chill.

'It's just as well,' mentioned Sogfort when they stopped to rest one afternoon, 'because we are nearly out of potatoes. From now on it must be craulberries.'

These were the size of passionfruit, with a tough, dark-blue skin, and each separate vine, twining over lower branches, produced ones that tasted different to any others. They mimicked grape, orange, pear, and so on, but had flavours, too, that were blends of these, or entirely their own.

Wolves had been scarce among the blackened trees. Now they reappeared, and Graf was kept busy each evening sketching family portraits.

He heard things from the wolves while he was doing this, for hardly anyone can resist chatting while having their portrait sketched.

'There was a great flood, not long ago,' the wolves told him. 'In our opinion it was the work of the Grand Knight, who plans to invade the forest in order to enslave all wolves. We are valuable to them for pulling their war chariots. But we shall flee from those clanking creatures, into realms of darkness. They underestimate our sense of smell and our speed.'

When Pinguel reported this to Sogfort, the owl merely shook his head.

TWENTY-SEVEN ~~~

It was on their third night of eating craulberries that Pinguel, now accustomed to long-distance climbing and swinging through trees, and no longer quite so exhausted, began to ask about their quest. All the owl had told him, and had repeated since, was that they were off to find allies for the blats.

'That boy, Hugo,' Sog elaborated as they prepared for bed. 'The famous golfer. He is a friend to blats. In his own way, he is extremely powerful.'

'The doll . . .'

'A real blat. Yes, I watched the match. The doll is a senior officer in the Great Forest's Spear Guard. And someone else, Pinguel. You may have read of him in all your study. Peregrine, the wizard. Or should I say, Peregrine the greatest wizard who ever was. We must find him too. You, he and Hugo are our world's only hope. Yes, you must join with them, Pinguel. You are a point of this triangle. Together, the three of you could accomplish much. But soon, soon —' Sogfort hooted this word like the owl he was — 'we must travel into the world beyond the forest, and that will not be easy. I have not been a part of it for many, many years. But enough talk. Let us sleep.'

TWENTY-EIGHT

They had no need of a compass, for the sun rose ahead of them as they journeyed through the morning, then passed across the sky to their left, and set at their backs.

Pinguel began to dream of branches rushing out of shadows, faster and faster, until they blurred together and he began to fall.

'I have scouted over the past weeks,' Sog confessed on their eighteenth day of travel, 'and this direction seemed the shortest. I flew high on clear days and looked through a telescope. Perhaps I was wrong. Perhaps I chose the longest way, by mistake. I knew the forest was deep, but *this* deep . . .' He shrugged.

'Why did we not travel over Dragon's Tooth?' Pinguel wondered. 'My mother came that way, didn't she?'

'She had help from some of the crab beetles, who live there. But in the years since then the crab beetles have given themselves over to strife and conflict. They wage civil wars, keep to their cracks, and refuse to speak to strangers.'

Three mornings later, Pinguel awoke to hear Sogfort calling down.

'Up here, boy. Come and see the limit of the forest, and beyond.'

With hands hardened to calluses on his palms and finger joints, the rubber soles of his shoes nearly worn through, and Madam's knitted jacket tied by its arms around his waist, the boy climbed. Sogfort was perched on a branch higher than the neighbouring trees. Pinguel jumped up beside him.

Short of the horizon the trees abruptly gave way to greyness and sharp-cornered, black shapes with high chimneys trailing clouds that looked like long pennants.

'Castles,' murmured the owl. 'Knights' castles. We will avoid them, if we can. Today will be our last full day of travel through the forest.'

TWENTY-NINE ~~~

Soon there were paths between the trees so wide that Sog and Pinguel could see right down to the forest floor.

'Many different smells,' Graf reported excitedly at lunchtime. He had called them down because the ground, he promised, was free of wolves. 'None for miles,' he stated, glancing around as though he hardly believed this himself.

That night they slept near the base of a tree, with Graf as sentry. And as Pinguel settled himself into a fork, with Sogfort perched just above, both no longer grabbing or climbing, or flapping wings, but still and silent, they began to hear a deep, crashing noise. Pinguel thought of towering metal hammers, of drills plunging into rock, of boulders smashing one against the other in a slow avalanche — all softened by distance into a murmur that was almost soothing.

After an hour's travel the next morning, the trees began to dwindle. Branches were broken off, jagged at their ends, and the paths became black mud through which Graf carefully picked his way. (Sog had warned him to keep an eye out for traps.) They came to a high, rusty wire fence, full of holes, at which Sogfort merely shook his head.

'An ancient attempt,' he explained, 'to keep wolves away from humans. Built before the days of the questing knights.'

They had come to the end of the forest.

The land stretched out, flat and muddy. They chose a path away from the knights' castles. Sogfort flew high to scout, then swooped to perch on Graf's shoulder.

'I'll stay here if you don't mind. Don't worry about walking in any particular way. I can keep my balance.'

Graf hardly noticed the owl, who, anyway, weighed next to nothing.

The earth was grey-brown, and faded into chilly mist on the horizon. Pinguel's hands and feet kept expecting to reach for a branch.

Graf padded behind, bag around neck swinging from side to side, owl on shoulder especially nervous at not having tree trunks around him, branches and leaves above.

As the sun began to set, they ate craulberries that they had picked before leaving the forest, and drank water. Just before nightfall, a mist rolled towards them. They found a hollow beside the path.

'We'll sleep here for the night.' Sogfort pointed, trying to sound cheerful. 'It'll be cold when the mist reaches us, so we'll have to huddle together.'

They got themselves as comfortable as they could as the mist swirled damply around them.

THIRTY ~~

'Things weren't always as bad as this,' spoke Sog into the gloomy silence in an effort to cheer up his companions.

'This used to be fields, or so I've heard. There was a river not far away, long since dammed for industrial purposes.

'At one stage of his life Peregrine the wizard lived — unless I'm mistaken — not far from where we are now.

'He had a cottage, and used to spend most of his time in a comfortable chair, feet on the windowsill, reading and taking notice of changes in the weather. One day he found himself pacing about his drawing room. Something was missing. Despite having his books and plenty of food, despite all his talent as a wizard, and the fact that he was in good health, he lacked something. The cottage suddenly seemed small and, despite its comfortable furniture, bare. So he set out along the very same path that we were following just now. Except that in those days — not so long ago, yet not so recent either — it was a broad highway, busy with merchants, timber cutters, and people on their way to visit relatives and friends.'

Sogfort waited.

'Go on,' asked Graf and Pinguel together.

Satisfied, the owl resumed.

'So the wizard found himself on a busy road, standing perfectly still because he had been struck by the knowledge of what it was that he lacked. He had to step to one side to avoid being run over by a speeding limousine, and then he screwed up his eyes with pain, because his foot had landed on something sharp and hard enough to push against the sole of his sandal and into his heel.

'He looked down, and saw a little grey stone. He picked it up and, as cars and buses, coaches and bicycles whizzed past, he found himself, a grown wizard, talking to the stone.

'"*You*," he accused. "You are what I have been missing. And it's been the same for you, I suspect, here by the side of the road. For what ever happens to a little grey stone? Who ever takes an interest? Who stops to talk?"

'And so he took the little stone, which to an ignorant observer had nothing remarkable about it, back to his cottage, and then who can say exactly what happened? All I know is the result — whether achieved by spells and suchlike, or simply by a friendly chat about nothing in particular. However it happened, the stone began to talk, and soon discovered that, after all, it had arms and legs, and longish hair that it tossed this way and that when nodding or shaking his head. True, his skin remained bluish-grey, and he could never help giving a shudder at the sight of sand (every grain of which was once a part of a stone), but for all the dullness of his past the grey stone became the perfect companion for Peregrine the wizard. For that, my dear fellow travellers, was what the wizard had been missing.'

The owl's story had its intended effect. The soothing notes of his voice blunted the strangeness around them, and soon the travellers were fast asleep in their hollow beside the path that had once been a busy road.

THIRTY-ONE ~~

The distant crash of machinery had been with them for too long for them to notice it any longer. Yet on waking up, and shivering at the early morning cold, they did hear the thump of horses' hooves and the clank of armour.

They stood still for just long enough to identify where the noise was coming from.

'Hop onto my back, Pinguel,' whispered Graf.

Before the travellers could move, though, confident that the sounds were coming from ahead, a voice called from behind:

'Halt, travellers, in the name of Lord Pinchie's Knights of Work!'

And out of the fog came a horse's hoof, then a grey corner of the leather barding that the animal wore for protection. In the stirrup was a metal foot; above this a leg, also of metal. At each jerk of the stirrup, causing the knee to bend, jets of steam escaped from pneumatic joints. To Pinguel, the knight was a true giant, like those in the legends that Madam read out on Thursday nights.

There were soon two others behind this first one, then three more soon joined them.

The knights had no faces, only metal visors with slits for eyes, and a patch of grille-work over the mouth. The horses blew out jets of steamy air from their nostrils, adding to the fog.

'Lo!' cried the knight who had arrived first, his voice as empty of feeling as a loudspeaker announcement. 'Show me your cards.' He held out a metal hand.

'What cards, O illustrious knight?' asked Sog, sounding not at all frightened.

'Clanka-clanka.' Like the sound of metal plates falling onto a stone floor, laughter clattered around them.

'BT Cards!' called out another knight, voice deeper than the first. 'Breathing Tax! Hurry! We cannot waste our time on such as you.'

'We are immigrants!' Sogfort had to raise his voice above the stamping and snorting of the horses (as Graf tensed his muscles, preparing to spring away, and

Pinguel held on tight). 'We come from afar. As soon as we reach a town we shall get jobs, earn money, and pay the tax.'

The knights were silent.

'Permission to proceed granted!' announced the knight who had spoken first. 'Be warned, immigrants, we shall alert all squads, and tell the officials of the Employment Bureau to expect you. If you have not paid your Breathing Tax within a week, no more air for you!'

The foremost knight reared his horse as though to stamp on them, then jerked the reins to one side and galloped away, giving brief life to the air with clods of earth and the clamour of armour.

'Breathing Tax,' huffed Graf scornfully as the early morning returned to silence.

'A joke, I suppose,' Pinguel muttered.

Sog only shook his head.

'We aren't really going to the town, are we?' the boy persisted.

'We can talk as we travel,' was all that Sog answered.

Pinguel continued on Graf's back, and the owl joined him, perching behind.

'Yes, we must go to the city,' Sog continued, once they were moving. From time to time he half stuck out a wing to keep his balance. 'A really huge city will give us our best chance of hearing of the whereabouts of Hugo, the golfing champion, and perhaps of Peregrine too. For it is in cities that news and rumour thrive. Besides, we will not get far beyond the forest without Tax Cards.'

A sloping line of darkness appeared through the mist: the corner of a pyramid that stood as high as a five-storey building. On each side was a medallion-like sculpture, half standing out, of a man with a long face, wearing a crown and a cloak. In scrolly writing around the edges were the words:

'Hail to Lord Duke Pinchie du Henderson, Preserver of the Peace, Purifier of the Air, Protector of the Free.'

THIRTY-TWO ~~~

A whining sound, then a single wheel came out of the mist, followed by a seated, brown bear holding a steering wheel. Behind him was the body of a truck heaped high with hay. The bear showed no surprise as he glanced at the wolf, owl and titan.

'Greetings!' called out Sog. 'How far to the city?'

'Two kilometres,' the bear answered in a voice that must have been deep even for bears.

Then he was gone into the mist.

A shack made of planks and squares of tin appeared, a wolf beside it pinning a sheet to a washing line. She called out:

'Dreadful weather!'

'They find nothing surprising about us,' Pinguel whispered. And as he spoke he realised why this must be. 'Yet' — he added — 'on the TV we see only humans, hardly ever a merryn. I had thought this world would be all humans.'

The shacks of plank and metal joined up to make one long building. Ahead was a bridge. A barge towed others, piled with coal, underneath it. At a crossroads a convoy of trucks rushed past, its after-draught nearly toppling Sog and Pinguel from Graf's back.

As the buildings grew taller, concrete and brick replaced plank and metal. Soon the titan and wolf saw their first human (except for on TV): a woman carrying a wicker basket of what looked like huge red berries to a shallow box that was tilted to face the road.

'Apples,' Sog explained. 'We're coming to a market.'

They turned a corner, then another, into a district crowded with humans, and stalls of oranges, potatoes, cherries, chestnuts, and many other things.

A small creature came towards them, carrying a bicycle wheel in both hands and a bunch of yellow flowers under one arm.

'A merryn,' whispered Pinguel, although the figure looked even smaller than on TV.

'Pears fresh from the coast!' called out a bear. 'Two credits a kilo!'

'Oranges from afar!' barked a wolf, in competition. 'One credit a bucket!'

The merryns operated smaller stalls, hung by chains from the supporting beams of verandahs and reached by means of rope ladders. They were selling jewellery, watches, microcassette recorders, and other items that, with their tiny fingers, they specialised in making and repairing.

'The imperial city of Vizzencourt,' Sog explained, 'in all its magnificence. We're looking for a place called the Hotel Parma, not all that magnificent. I knew the father of the owner, once.'

Outside a cafe, a merryn with a narrow face and bright, observant eyes stared at Pinguel, blinked, and stared even harder. He called something to the human behind the counter, and set off after the three travellers.

As he rounded the next corner, Graf sniffed and looked back. Something was wrong. But no ... only the usual crowd behind them.

When Graf started moving again, the merryn stepped from a shadow and resumed his following. Meanwhile, the human in the cafe telephoned the number the merryn had given him.

They followed a side street, and went up a staircase beneath a neon sign.

'Mr Sogfort! Can it be?' cried a huge human woman, plucking the owl from Graf's back and holding him close to her, yet gently, in the crook of her arm, like a baby. 'What a pleasure! No, what an *honour*, after all these years. I remember still, and so well, those nights that you and my father stayed up late, having conversations. And your friends' — she nodded with solemn politeness — 'are welcome too. Most welcome.'

When Sogfort had smoothed down his feathers, he enquired after the woman's parents and grandparents, then hovered a little distance behind as she led them all to a room that contained three human-sized beds.

'And I am afraid...' She gave a shrug that explained, *I am forced to do this.* 'I must see your Breathing Tax Cards, or I am not allowed to give you a room.'

Sog explained that they would have the cards by tomorrow.

Once they were alone, Pinguel shook his head.

'How did the world ever get to be so dreadful?'

Graf had curled up on his bed. Now he stretched his legs and yawned. It was he, after all, who had done all the walking.

Sog flew to a sink in the corner, washed his face, then lowered his beak to scoop up water, tipping his head back for it to flow down his throat.

'My dear Pinguel.' He reached for a towel. 'You may be cleverer than I am, but you are impatient. I know, for I have studied you carefully these past years. I have watched you, day after day. Before you judge this place, wait until you have seen more of it. After all, it may turn out to be even worse.'

Outside the Hotel Parma, the merryn-follower took careful note of the address, and hurried away.

THIRTY-THREE ~~~

The next morning a wind pushed the mist up, changing it to grey cloud. Sog flapped his wings, and Pinguel, sitting on Graf's back, held on tight to the bristly fur as they set off down the lane, heading for the city centre.

At the foot of the main steps of the Central Employment Bureau stood a truck with twelve birds in the back tray, behind chicken wire, grey blankets the size of human handkerchiefs around their shoulders.

The birds had no feathers. Their skin was pink and along their foreheads were wrinkles of worry that no one, normally, would have been able to see.

'What are you staring at?' demanded one, catching sight of the travellers, who had halted in surprise.

'We sold our feathers,' lamented another, before anyone could reply.

From their curved-over beaks they looked to be a sort of parrot.

'Sold your —?' began Graf and Pinguel.

Another bird stalked over. 'To pay Breathing Tax. But do not blame or feel sorry for us. Now we have permanent vouchers. We never need pay again. How do *you* get the credits to pay?'

'Come, we must hurry,' whispered Sog.

Inside the Bureau, people, merryns and animals were queuing at barred windows. In the middle was a booth with a sign — BIRTHDAYS — above a little man sharpening a pencil with great concentration.

They waited behind a female bear with two small cubs. When they reached the window the man behind it stammered:

'I-immigrants? So, what can you do?' He stared at Pinguel, then at the little satchel around Graf's neck. A sketchpad and a stick of charcoal stuck out the top.

'I have some experience in growing potatoes,' mentioned Sog reflectively.

The man pushed a form beneath the grille, glancing again at Pinguel.

'Fill this out and take it to Lodgement, next door.'

'I am a portrait painter,' Graf answered, more than a touch of pride in his voice.

The man pushed across another form.

Before Pinguel could speak, Sog said:

'And this is an assistant portrait painter. Any master painter, such as Graf here, needs an assistant in order to do his job with the required degree of beauty.'

'What?' The man looked doubtful.

'Put him down as another portrait painter. They work as a team,' Sog suggested.

The man blinked, and pushed across a form to Pinguel.

'Be sure to take these to Lodgement. Next.'

The new arrivals filled out their forms and took them to another window, where they were finally given their Breathing Tax vouchers and the addresses where they were required to report for work.

It was at this window, facing a woman with grey hair and a not unkindly face, that Pinguel, having jumped the merryn-stairs to the counter, asked as she stamped the date on the BT vouchers:

'We're from out of town. Please, what happens if you *don't* pay Breathing Tax?'

'Why, you aren't allowed to breathe.'

'But how do they stop you?'

She banged down the stamp.

'There are many ways to stop a person from breathing. But the air has to be kept clean, doesn't it? Free of dust, smoke, and poisonous gases? And that costs money, lots of money. So isn't it fair that those who get the benefit, by breathing nice, fresh air, should help to pay for it? And if anyone refuses to pay, should they be allowed to breathe it for free, while others do pay?'

Before Pinguel could say anything, the woman had looked to the people behind them. 'Next!'

When the friends were reunited that evening, they were exhausted not from work but from more hours waiting in queues and filling out forms. Only at the very end of the day had Graf and Pinguel, at the Bureau of Artists, been issued with Guild Membership Forms (after signing many official documents) and told where to report for work the next morning.

Sog had fared no better.

'But I did get to talk to some falcons, who told me why those hawks and eagles were speared a few weeks ago, over Deep Forest. Refusal to pay tax. A recent edict, from the Council of the Grand Duke, states that due to the fact that air currents circulate with a sad lack of self-control, all creatures on the planet, wherever they live, must henceforth pay Breathing Tax. The edict specifically mentions Deep Forest. The birds were shot by guided arrows fired from jet aircraft.'

'Including Deep Forest,' wondered Graf.

'And I heard about Hugo, too,' added the owl. 'The police want to question him about rumours that he cheated in the World Championships. He's on the run, they say. No one can find him. I will try to discover more tomorrow.'

That night, Pinguel felt as if he were sinking in an ocean of homesickness. It did not surprise him that the tax had been extended to the forest. Why not make the trees pay it? He thought of Cliffkin and Madam, and how much he would rather have been with them, tonight.

THIRTY-FOUR ~~

A murmuring crowd filled the footpath, spilling into the hotel lane. A crunching noise came from the road.

'We must work for at least a month,' Sog had explained over breakfast, 'to pay tax and obtain passports, otherwise further travel will be impossible.'

He flew to a lamp post, while Graf nuzzled between human and bear legs, Pinguel sitting astride his back.

'Aaaah,' sighed the crowd.

Pinguel glimpsed white-tipped paws ahead, then heard Graf mutter:

'I know those wolves.'

A team of sixteen was straining against harnesses, leather-jerkinned merryns with whips astride their backs. The animals moved slowly, pushing back at the road with powerful hind legs, tongues lolling out of their mouths, as they dragged a huge log, stripped of its branches and bark and resting on wagons made of sliced-off log ends and branches.

Clanking and hissing next filled the street, as a detachment of knights approached.

Craning, Pinguel peered further down. Behind the knights were more wolves, and another huge log, the whole procession dwindling into the distance.

'Wolves from Deep Forest,' Graf said as they followed a side street. 'Belonging to a pack not far from mine.'

'But how could knights have caught wolves who come from so deep in the forest?' Pinguel asked Sog, keeping his voice low as they passed a group of bears.

'I do not know,' the owl answered. 'This is happening much faster than I thought. I knew it would be soon, but not this soon.' He continued quickly: 'Are you all right, Pinguel? Can you hear me?'

'Yes, Sog. I hear you.'

The owl looked small and old, perched on Graf's back. Pinguel thought:

'Sog doesn't know what's happening. None of us, really, knows much about this world.'

Graf and Pinguel entered a square that turned out to be deserted except for a handful of merryns, in grey coats and carrying briefcases, bustling across a far corner. The merryn who had spotted them the day before yesterday watched from a shadow behind a tree. Two knights stood motionless in sentry boxes either side of a wide gateway. Glancing frequently at the slip of paper they had been given at the Artists' Bureau, Pinguel found their address: a metal door with '39' painted on it.

An old, merryn woman appeared in the gap, standing on tiptoes as she pulled a rope that, through a system of pulleys, opened the human-sized door.

'Quick,' she commanded. 'Can't hold it for long. Step back or you'll be squashed. That's it. You'll be the new portrait painters. This way.'

She led them down a corridor to a room with a counter piled with brushes and paints at merryn height.

'Take what you want. Make sure you sign the receipts book.' She glanced at the clock. 'Eight. Better hurry. You could be called any minute.' She gave Pinguel a close look, then laughed as she picked up a metal bucket and mop and walked off. 'Well, good luck.'

Paintbrushes, paints and sticks of charcoal were arranged on shelves in neat stacks. Wooden frames with canvas stretched across them leaned against a wall, longing to be painted on.

'Everyone seems to look at me —' began Pinguel, but Graf interrupted:

'Every size of brush!' He looked around. 'Who are we supposed to paint?'

Pinguel had sat down on a crate of linseed oil.

'I wish I'd never left the forest. The blats aren't safe. I just know it. And everyone looks at me as if they already knew me.'

He pulled his thickly woven jacket more tightly around his shoulders.

A tallish merryn appeared in the door and exclaimed:

'Well, well, *well*!' He was staring at Pinguel. He had shoulder-length grey hair and wore a dark blue robe that went all the way to the floor. 'And who might you be, merryn?'

'My name is Pinguel,' the boy began, 'and this is . . .'

The merryn cut him off with a wave of a hand. 'No, no . . . your *last* name?'

'De Mandiargues.'

'Hmm, and they say you're a portrait painter. Well, come along then.' The man gave a thin smile. 'And what are you doing here, animal?'

'I'm —' Graf began.

'He's the portrait painter,' Pinguel interrupted. 'I'm his assistant.'

'Assistant to a wolf? How curious. Well, I'm an assistant too, in a manner of speaking. Nothing wrong with that. Yes, some of the greatest creatures in the world start off as assistants. Come along, both of you. Bring sketchpads and charcoal. That's all. Come along.'

Graf tucked the materials into his bag. The corridors were low and dark, with Graf having to crouch to get through doorways, then they broadened and became higher, with spotless white walls, chandeliers lit by candle-shaped electric bulbs, and marble floors that, after only a minute or two of walking, became red carpet.

A knight stood either side of a golden doorway. They glanced down, saw the old merryn, and one pushed half the door open.

The room beyond was the largest Pinguel or Graf had ever imagined, let alone seen. Even for a human it was enormous.

The walls were covered with paintings, and down the centre was a red carpet leading to another door. The paintings all appeared (they couldn't see the ones further down) to be of one person, or merryn.

Graf glanced at several of these, then at Pinguel, who was standing perfectly still.

The person in the painting had long, black hair and green eyes. His chin came to a narrow point and his cheekbones were high. If he spoke, you couldn't help feeling, it would be with a husky, deep voice.

'Why,' Graf whispered, 'it's *you*.'

'Interesting, don't you agree?' murmured the merryn, rubbing his hands together. 'Hurry, or we shall be late.'

'Me,' Pinguel whispered, feeling light-headed.

And all the paintings, as they followed the red carpet, were of this one person. They showed the man alone, standing or sitting, wearing armour or ordinary clothes, a rich variety of cloaks, sometimes a crown ... or riding on the back of an eagle, or wolf, or showed him human-sized alone on horseback or accompanied by a troop of knights. One painting had him with his arm around a smiling, white snake who was wearing a red cape and had a golden crown on its head.

The only change in the man himself, as they progressed down the hall, was that he grew older. By halfway down, grey had seeped into his hair, then lines appeared around his eyes and mouth, and a fold of flesh, then two folds, drooped beneath his chin. By the end of the hall his hair was white and his face positively sagged.

The door at the end was as huge and golden as the first.

'This way,' muttered the merryn. 'Less formal.'

He touched the corner of a picture frame, and a small doorway appeared beneath.

They climbed stairs, and found themselves in a light-filled room, a sort of observatory, with the roof and two of the walls made of glass. A throne with its back facing the door stood among graceful pot plants, armchairs, and an easel. All the objects were merryn-sized, which made the room look even huger.

'Bow,' whispered the merryn, lowering his head. Then he called out, louder:

'Greetings, Your Excellency!'

Someone got up from the throne. Wearing a cloak made of rows of beautifully bright colours that shimmered and glinted as they caught and lost the light, he pointed to the horizon.

'See that ugly smoke over there, Lord Chamberlain?'

'Yes, Your Excellency.'

'It comes from Deep Forest. Smoke.'

'Yes, Your Excellency.'

The man turned, though with the light behind him his face remained in darkness. His shoulder-length hair was white, and he wore dark blue trousers, a black shirt, and polished black boots that came all the way to his knees.

He stood in silence, staring.

'Who are these?'

'The portrait painters, your Ex—'

'No. Names.'

'Well, the merryn's name is Pinguel, the wolf's . . .'

'Not the wolf,' interrupted the man, who had taken a couple of steps closer. 'Where do you come from, boy? Let me confess something. My spies have been watching you. I ordered that you be directed here, no matter what your occupation. Please do not lie to me. Where do you come from?'

The voice was so used to giving orders and to being obeyed that Pinguel found himself answering, as he had done on the forms at the Employment Bureau:

'A village —'

'A village near Deep Forest? Well, well.' The old merryn — if that is what he was — took another step and, now accustomed to the abrupt shadings of light and dark in the room, Pinguel made out the details of his face, although the eyes remained in darkness.

It was the man from the portrait gallery, even older than in the most recent of the paintings.

'Aha.' He gave a short laugh, while waving an arm at his Lord Chancellor. 'Go.'

When the merryn had closed the door behind him, the lord, or whoever he was, waved an arm at the chairs. 'Let us sit down.

'So,' he began, glancing from Graf (crouching with front legs out, like a sphinx, on the floor) to Pinguel. 'From a little village near Deep Forest. Well, well. Your parents, who are they? Let me guess. A simple washerwoman, married to a woodcutter? Or a farming couple, the fingernails of the father mostly black with soil, those of the woman usually dusted with flour from baking bread — and sometimes from those biscuits, too, that she likes to decorate with dribbles of pink icing? Is that the case, my dear fellow?'

Before Pinguel could answer, having no idea what he was going to say, Graf spoke:

'We came to paint a portrait, Your Excellency.'

'Oh, Mr Wolf. I am sorry. I forgot about you.' He turned back to Pinguel. 'My point is, the truth is more interesting than lies. You have just been through my portrait gallery. Do you know something? I fascinate myself. And did you notice something about those portraits, my young near-forest dweller?'

'Yes, I did.'

'And what might that have been?'

'They were all of you.' Pinguel had a feeling that he was walking along a narrow bridge that had no handrails, and below was only dangerous unknown. He could only stay on the bridge by being extremely careful of what he said.

'They were all of me,' the man repeated. 'And of you too. We look alike, don't we?'

'Yes.'

'Do you know my name? It is Grand Duke Pinchie — Pinchie to you — du Henderson. I am a ruler. I am *the* ruler.'

For an instant, the duke covered his eyes with a hand.

'My childhood,' he resumed, 'was lonely. Pay attention, since you are portrait painters. For loneliness I favour blue shading into grey. Suggest a cold wind by having leaves point in a single direction. Since then I have,' he raised his hands as though to show that they were empty, 'shocked myself.

'I have grown old. Do you know one of the most important parts of a portrait painting, or of a photograph for that matter? Come here, boy.'

The duke led Pinguel to a window. They were higher than the rest of Vizzencourt, and looked down on streets, squares, and the roofs of other buildings.

The duke put a hand on Pinguel's shoulder. 'See how tiny creatures look from up here? Like each of those specks down there, I am growing old. One day I shall die. Like everything, I am temporary.'

He faced Pinguel.

'But I am different. I plan to be permanent. Come with me.'

The duke led Pinguel to a doorway, then to a smaller room. He flicked a switch and lights came on around a single painting, a full-length portrait of a woman in a purple dress. In one hand she held a sword, its blade cradled over the crook of her other arm. Around her was forest, the leaves all pointing in one direction.

'My wife. She left me, and died. She did not share my view of the world.'

Pinguel stared. The woman was beautiful in a way that was both distant in terms of strangeness, yet near in terms of feeling. She might have been thinking of a joke, one that would sound solemn when first spoken but which would quickly, no matter who tried to halt it, break into laughter.

He remembered Deep Forest, and the wolves he had just seen, dragging logs. Where was Cliffkin now?

'I lived near Deep Forest,' he began, a lump in his throat. He had no idea what he was going to say next, he just spoke. 'The wolves, for instance, seemed happier when I knew them, than when I saw them this morning, dragging logs.'

'Yes!' cried the duke. 'You look like me, and you think like me. I suppose you are strong, too, like me. But I trust you. And I rarely make a mistake, when I trust. Now listen to me, and I will explain.

'Creatures hate change, so before I can improve their lives, they must first become a touch unhappy. Some creatures — you may be surprised to learn — even resist my Knights of Work. It happened recently, inside Deep Forest. Small creatures like us, with slightly longer noses. Called blats, I believe. Fled from us into their treetops, they did. Wonderful at hiding, and at first my officers had no idea where they were. But we invaded in force. I doubt if they even knew what the word "force" meant before they encountered us. They threw spears and fired arrows with accuracy and skill.' The duke's face clouded over. 'A few of my knights were scratched. So these particular blats, I am sorry to say, must be punished.' He glanced at a wristwatch. 'In Execution Square. Why don't you accompany me, and see for yourself?'

The duke pulled a cord by the door.

'Your friend can have the rest of the day off. An execution is a gloomy spectacle, at best, but every country finds them necessary, from time to time, either in the form of life-taking or life-imprisoning. Here, let us take these stairs. We shall go onto the roof, and travel by helicopter.

'To be kind,' he went on, 'often it is necessary to be cruel. By punishing a few blats, I teach others to be happy.'

THIRTY-FIVE ~~~

The helicopter swung across the city, and even the upward soar of the machine could add nothing to the ache in Pinguel's heart. He remembered both Cliffkin and Sog warning him against impulsiveness. Yet, *executions*.

He grabbed the metal edges of his seat, which vibrated with the noisy motor.

How was it that the duke looked so much like him?

Was he a titan too?

As the helicopter swooped towards the outskirts of the city, Pinguel forced himself to be calm. 'Make the wisest decision,' he urged himself, 'not merely the one that you think of first.'

The helicopter descended towards a white circle on a rooftop. In a square beside the building was a huge crowd of — from this height — specks.

Quickly the specks became humans, with, behind them, merryns on raised platforms. To one side stood a wolf-pack: iron-foundry labourers on their lunchbreak, fur singed above the line of the gloves they wore near the furnaces. Everyone was facing a stage made of wooden planks yellow in their freshness and guarded by a ring of Knights of Work.

Here stood six more knights in a group, and a tall human who wore a black cowl with large eyeholes and, despite the weather (no doubt in order to display his huge muscles), no shirt.

Knights cleared a space for the helicopter to land, then a path to the platform.

'I predict,' murmured Pinchie, 'that you will observe my power, and join me. We are one, you and I.'

Pinguel focused on the duke's colourful robe, and decided that it was made not of cloth (although it might have been silk at a distance), but from the vanes, sewn together, of birds' feathers. Then he recalled the parrots outside the Employment Bureau who had sold their feathers to gain exemption from Breathing Tax.

As they crossed the square the crowd fell silent. Pinguel glimpsed a human staring with his mouth open, a golden ring swaying back and forth through the lobe of one ear.

As they climbed the ramp a chilly breeze struck them in the face, and Pinguel caught a whiff of baked bread.

The duke raised his hands to the crowd.

When everyone cried out, their voices combined to make one voice:

'Hail! Hail! Hail!'

'Let the executions begin!' cried the duke.

Pinguel stepped back to see the cowled man-giant, the executioner, take from a knight, standing in shadow behind him, a cage containing what at first sight looked like several merryns. Hands tied behind backs, they were unable to balance as the cage swayed, and staggered against a side.

The cage contained five blats.

Pinguel recognised them as they pitched towards him, twisting around to break their fall against the bars. Members of the Spear and Arrow Guards and ...

Ogren. His childhood friend, Ogren, was leaning into the nearer corner, face pressing against the wire, one ear red with blood, and he was staring at Pinguel, eyes wide with terror and — now — surprise too.

A flock of birds passed overhead, their shadows darkening the platform, but no one except the duke (who scowled) paid any attention, they were so transfixed by the seriousness of what was about to happen.

Behind the executioner was a pole with a bar at the top, making a T shape, and from each side hung three nooses made of silken rope.

The executioner opened the door of the cage and reached for the first blat.

Time had slowed down. Tendons passed across the executioner's elbow joint as he bent his arm. Pinguel remembered his golf shot at the Bardles, and Cliffkin's warning never to let the blats know his strength. And he had kept his secret so thoroughly that he had managed hardly ever to think of it himself.

And Pinguel suspected that Pinchie had made a terrible mistake. Just because they looked alike, because (the possibility was growing at the back of Pinguel's mind) they were related, did not mean that Pinguel would hold the same beliefs. As for strength, was it possible that Pinchie realised exactly what Pinguel was capable of doing?

The boy knew that the executioner must not get his hand around a blat, while at the same time he must not be allowed to drop the cage. A fall from that height would kill a blat.

And then (the hand moving closer, closer) there were the six Knights of Work on the platform, and Duke Pinchie too.

The duke, he sensed, although an old man, was the greatest danger.

So the boy (who was nearly fully grown, anyway, only half a head shorter than the duke) took a step back, and pushed the illustrious ruler in the chest, so that he tumbled off the platform.

The crowd fell utterly silent, then shrieked with a mixture of surprise, horror and delight.

Pinguel, meanwhile, had darted over, grabbed the heel of the executioner's boot and pushed it forward.

His strength shocked him. He even had to pull the boot back a bit, not to send the man flying off the platform.

As he fell, the executioner let go of the cage, and all the knights rushed for Pinguel.

The boy — or titan — jumped over so that he was beneath the cage, dodged one knight, and gave another a kick into the one coming from the opposite direction. The joints of their pneumatic armour hissed desperately as they each tried to stop. The collision itself sounded like a hundred cymbal-clashes compressed into two seconds.

Pinguel grabbed a toe of the next one's armour, twisted it, and sent the knight cartwheeling off the platform.

The cage containing six blats, now that he was using all his strength and had forgotten to pretend to be weak, felt as if it hardly weighed anything.

As he gently put it down, and tore open the door, he glimpsed the huge crowd around the platform. A bald man raised a fist, and laughed. Knights on horseback were attempting to rush in, but found their progress blocked by the throng.

People had begun to shout encouragement. Now their voices sharpened to a howl of warning, as a knight from the back of the platform raised a sword to crash it onto the titan.

Pinguel shoved the knight backwards, off the platform.

And now the crowd fell silent. For Duke Pinchie, taking huge strides for such a small creature, white hair half covering his face and his beautiful cloak hanging from one shoulder, was climbing the ramp.

As Pinguel noticed the faces looking up, arms pointing skywards too, Ogren bumped against him, and a familiar voice came from overhead.

'Quick! Look up! Stand apart!'

Hair flew across faces. The platform shook.

The voice belonged to Sog. There were more birds with him: hawks, wings beating frantically.

Pinguel and the blats moved far enough apart for the birds to come down, until claws grasped their chests, and, before Duke Pinchie could reach the platform, they were all lifted high with the noise of wings beating and air rushing past their ears.

Except for one furious roar, that of the duke:

'Come back! You will never escape! You betrayed me! Call the Airforce!'

PART SIX

Execution Square was on the outskirts of the city. Keeping low to save energy, the birds raced over rooftops until they came to farming land, then to a line of trees along a creek. A wind whistled warnings through bare twigs. Blats and titan found themselves on a mossy bank. Neither strong enough to carry anyone, nor fast enough to keep up even with the burdened hawks, Sog arrived seconds later, out of breath.

As Pinguel untied the blats' wrists, one of the hawks laughed.

'I remember you! I do. The short-nosed blat child who feared nothing.'

He turned to his six fellow hawks. 'The one I told you about, years ago. I caught him, but he grabbed my feathers, forced me to let go.'

'Peter the Hawk.' Pinguel noticed that his hands were trembling. A snowflake landed on the bird's beak. 'That's the name I gave you.'

'Peter?' The bird laughed in a kindly way. 'My name is Harth, actually.'

Hawks have a strange sense of humour. They found this confusion of names hilarious, and shrieked with laughter as the blats began to talk all at once, rubbing their wrists, thanking Pinguel and the birds as well as telling Pinguel what had happened in the forest:

'They came from aeroplanes. Middle of the night. Took everyone they could prisoner. Chained our ankles together to prevent an escape.'

'. . . burned down trees in a large circle . . .'

'...no stars or moon. Couldn't see a thing. When the alarm sounded ...'

'...according to Clerkwellstone, they probably found out about us by using rocket satellites, orbiting ...'

'Cliffkin? Fine' — this was Ogren — 'or as fine as anyone can be, after being made a slave. Madam?'

'I saw her,' put in a boy no older than Ogren, who had started to drop to his knees to drink from the stream. 'Taken off ahead of the others, to the work camp.'

'We,' put in a blat called Folthro, a senior cadet in the Arrow Guard with a nose long even for a blat, 'we *didn't* surrender.'

'No,' Ogren confirmed, though more thoughtfully, and with less pride about it. 'We kept on fighting. My father?' he answered before Pinguel could even ask the question. 'Injured. They took the injured away to be treated. I haven't seen him since. But —'

'Excuse me.' Sog flew to midstream, where the water was a cold, dark blue, and hovered there.

'We have not escaped! The Airforce will be here in minutes, and even hawks cannot outrun jet planes. Pinchie moves faster, and knows more, than I ever suspected. I suggest we split up. You' — he pointed to the blats — 'go back to the forest by different routes, and hide there. Pinguel, you must go over the Cold Mountains, to continue our quest. Yes, yes.' The hawks had started to protest, fluffing out their chest feathers with indignation. 'I know it's quite a feat, to fly over those mountains, and carry someone at the same time, but if none of you is prepared to do it, I'll have a try myself. But we must leave now. No further talk.'

The hawk, Harth, who had picked up Pinguel when he had been a toddler, murmured:

'If you'll allow me, young fellow, I'll have another go at carrying you. I know of a lowish pass, from my reckless days.'

'A-all right!' stammered Sog, sounding more frightened than Pinguel had ever heard him. 'Let us leave!' As the hawks hopped nearer, the owl shouted to Pinguel:

'Graf telephoned me at the Potato Centre, and told me what was happening. He's hiding, and will set off tonight for the forest.'

And then the hawks were off, each carrying a fugitive blat or titan, and heading in different directions to confuse any spy satellites that might be watching.

THIRTY-SEVEN ~~~

Piloted by Air Knights in silver flying suits, jets hurried to break the sound barrier, causing a boom that rattled the windows of every building in Vizzencourt. There were sixteen, of the latest design. More would follow, as crews of bears hurried to fill tanks, and knights hurried, zipping up suits, from barracks.

They searched for hawks and an owl. Heading for Deep Forest, the birds found it easy to avoid the planes; all they had to do was land in a tree, or in the shadow of a farm building, when they heard the roar.

It wasn't so easy for Pinguel and Harth. After the farmland around Vizzencourt came olive trees and sheep pasture, the grass pale brown and huddled into clumps from the cold, then ragged swamps, followed by fifteen long miles (at its shortest point) of that flat and featureless territory labelled on maps as 'The Frozen Wastes'.

Over the swamps, a jet shrieked behind them, and Harth landed in a tuft of grass and lowered his head. Pinguel jumped to crouch beneath a wing.

The jet passed overhead, leaving a vapour trail behind. When the sky was silent again, Harth took a deep breath, and muttered:

'Here we go.'

Pinguel climbed back on, the feathers feeling rougher than they looked.

Harth stretched out as he flew, and flicked his head from side to side at blink-of-eye speed. The ground changed from dull sheets of water (reflecting the sky) and mud, to greyish blue, with not even the straggliest clump of grass to provide cover.

The freezing air rushed so powerfully into Pinguel's face that, in order to see, he had to blink rapidly and hold a hand over his eyes. The Cold Mountains appeared to grow out of the earth, first bluish like The Frozen Wastes, then icy white with black streaks where snow and ice had slipped to expose rock beneath.

Harth's wings stroked the air.

One-handed, Pinguel did up the topmost buttons of his jacket, but it made little difference. Aided by the wind, the iciness raced up his sleeves, stung his ears, and made his fingertips ache as though he had slammed them in a door. Never had he experienced such cold.

He blinked to clear his eyes, and the world looked as if it had been up-ended. The mountains disappeared into cloud. Not one of them looked as if it would ever finish in a peak. Momentarily, this made him feel as if the duke

154

were watching him from high above, and he, Pinguel, really was nothing but a speck.

The mountains were so huge, they seemed about to speak. And for an instant it did occur to Pinguel that, after waiting for so many millions of years, the mountains had finally worked out what it was they wished to say.

It began as a tearing sound, a roar of outrage ... but before any words came out, Harth began to dive, calling to Pinguel:

'Jets!'

They were flying at high altitude, and what Pinguel had taken to be noise from the mountains was really the shriek of engines reflected back.

'If we can just make the foothills,' Harth cried.

Mounds of rock, rubble and snow from avalanches were heaped up at the base. Harth was moving his wings faster now, no longer stroking but beating the air. Then something whooshed past, too fast to see, causing what started out as a flash of orange and red, like a tropical flower, and slowed to become a fountain of snow and rock.

The jet had fired a missile.

Next, the plane chattered, and Pinguel noticed one of Harth's feathers whip loose, and up.

Travelling so fast that it threatened to crash into the mountains, the plane looped like a metal shaving, and became invisible among clouds as it veered around to make another pass.

'Hang on!' warned Harth.

Harth's left wing buckled near its tip, but he stuck it out and, with the good one, made sure they glided rather than fell.

155

They landed on a rock that jutted over loose stones. Harth slipped, and Pinguel grabbed him around the neck. He found it hard to stand, his head was spinning so badly from their spiralling dive. Harth dragged his damaged wing, as they crawled as far under the rock as they could. The air smelt fresh, and a little proud too: it was clear than no one had ever breathed it before. The jet roared twice more overhead.

A long minute after the jet's second pass, Pinguel started to move out.

'Wait. No.' Harth spoke in a strained voice, as though already partly frozen up. 'Don't. It will come again.'

'I don't care.' Pinguel was stamping his feet and waving his arms. 'Can you fly?' he asked the hawk.

Harth was silent, then hopped out, both wings tucked in but one still bent. 'Yes,' he gasped, 'but only in short bursts.' He glanced at the sheer slope behind them. 'And not that high. No.'

'All right.' Pinguel had never felt more determined. 'I'm stronger than I look. I'll climb the mountains, and go down the other side. If I can't climb them, I'll push them aside! You fly back to the forest. I'll get help, somehow, and see you there with the blats. But we'd better hurry before the jet comes.'

'Climb?' wondered Harth. He shook his head. 'No one has ever climbed these mountains. Even for birds it is difficult to get over them. Besides, there are monsters. I have seen them for myself. You must not —'

Pinguel was feeling quite at ease, now that he had made his decision. 'No, I've read of creatures doing more difficult things. Anyhow, no alternative: we'll freeze if we stay here.'

'We can travel back slowly, across the wastes.'

'No, Sog asked me to go over the mountains. Hugo must be there, or Peregrine the wizard. I'll see you at the forest, Harth.'

And with that, Pinguel set off.

He had gone about a hundred metres, and the mountains hadn't even begun to get steep, when ten jets raced overhead. They tore back and forth across the foothills for about five minutes as Pinguel lay huddled into shadow alongside a rock, shivering. When their noise had ceased, he jumped out, hopping up and down to get warmth back into his feet and hands, and looked downhill for Harth.

Just as he was about to turn away, he saw a brown speck hop, fly a few metres, and hop again, into The Frozen Wastes.

He resumed his climb. Everything was silent. Nature was taking a deep breath, astonished at what this boy was attempting.

'You *wo-o-o-on't* succeed,' a gust of wind remarked, whistling past jagged rocks.

The boy strode out, getting warmer, and just as he began to grow thirsty, he found snow in a hollow between two rocks. Pinguel fancied that he could detect the faintest possible tinge of blat strawberries, grown on uppermost platforms, and this reminded him of how much depended on the success of his journey.

He walked up and up, and when he came to a sheer cliff he found that his rubber-soled, cloth-topped blat boots, although worn from his journey through the forest, were ideal for fitting into the smallest of cracks.

He had the strength, also, to pull himself up with no more than two fingers of one hand.

When he began to feel hungry, and so suddenly that dizziness made him press a cheek against icy rock and breathe deeply, he told himself that he had often missed meals — off playing with Ogren, or visiting Clerkwellstone, Madam or Graf — and that lack of food would not be a problem for a long time to come.

And this was true. As he climbed, he forgot his hunger, and thought instead of life among the blats. Looking back, he could see all the way to the distant cluster of grey and brown buildings that was Vizzencourt.

THIRTY-EIGHT ~~~

As the sun set, shadows, like the ghosts of avalanches returning to their origins, crept up the mountainside. Distant farmland glowed rich green, then darkened as the lights of Vizzencourt came on.

Under cover of darkness, Sog and Graf, tired and hungry, and taking great care to avoid the numerous patrols of knights, made their way back to Deep Forest. Everything now depended on Pinguel. Sog cursed himself for not having left the forest with the boy far earlier; he had thought too much, and acted too late. Both owl and wolf felt too defeated to talk. On the outskirts of the forest itself, six tired hawks landed on upper branches, and blats climbed from their backs. They would rest here, and resume their journey towards the heart of the forest tomorrow.

Pinguel reached the snowline moments before being engulfed by the greatest darkness of all, before moonrise yet after the setting of the sun. He looked back at the lights of the city, and laughed. So what if it was dark and growing colder every second? He was hardly tired, and he had been right about the hunger: it had gone entirely. He was far stronger than he had suspected. His fight at the execution platform had proved that. He would climb all night and, who knows, by morning he might be over the summit. Then it would be warmer, and he would rest a while and enjoy the view.

As though sympathetic to the boy's confidence, the mountain soon finished with its cliff faces and rocky overhangs and became a simple (though steep) snowy slope.

THIRTY-NINE ~~~

The moon came out.

Pinguel climbed, and climbed.

He was light enough to walk across, without falling through, the snow's icy crust. Yet as he made his way he began to experience a type of loneliness that he had never felt before.

Now everything was up to him. His life with the blats seemed remote. The cold whispered: 'Those days are gone. There is no point trying to save them. They are gone forever. You cannot revive the past.'

He thought of his Thursday nights with Cliffkin, Faringaria, the chess pieces, and the other inhabitants of the desk drawers. Had there been time for Cliffkin to hide them? Without Thursday nights, and their conversations and games, and meals of syrup and sugar, the refugees would slide into deeper hibernation and — Cliffkin had warned — eventually into death.

'And so what?' whispered the cold darkness. 'Isn't that the fate of every living thing? So why not now, rather than later? What do seconds, minutes, even years matter, when in the end you will be with me anyway? So lie down, boy. You are tired. Rest awhile, just a short while, and soon you will find yourself comfortable forever.'

Trudging up, up, into greater and greater cold, Pinguel found himself remembering those snowflakes that he had watched falling through the forest. Down, down ... until always, sooner or later, they touched a tree or blat platform, and perished.

He thought of the paintings, back at the palace, of the man growing older. And the woman in the purple dress. Who had she been? He couldn't tell if he believed, or simply hoped, that she was his mother. As for the man, he dreaded that he might turn out to be his father.

'Lie down. Rest,' whispered the cold darkness.

Pinguel walked with his hands tucked into his sleeves for warmth. He stumbled, reached out, and felt nothing. He saw, or thought he could, his hand spread out against the moonlit snow, but could feel nothing. He touched his cheek.

Nothing.

He laughed with surprise. A ghost already? Was this the sort of dream that ghosts have?

To feel his living skin, to prove that he wasn't dead, he pushed his hand through the buttons of his jacket and beneath his shirt, and there, on the skin of his chest, he felt the touch of something icy — his own fingers.

He was freezing. He stamped his feet. No, he couldn't feel *them* either.

And now, more than ever in his life, he became frightened.

No one knew exactly where he was, and the world was being overtaken by Duke Pinchie, his Breathing Tax, and the Knights of Work. Pinguel again recalled the portrait of the woman who had looked so much like himself.

Could she have been his mother?

He stumbled, crawled a few metres, and picked himself up. Often he had tried and failed to remember his mother carrying him, a baby, into Deep Forest.

And now there was no Deep Forest left for refugees.

He stumbled again and again, yet continued to walk. Warmish stuff dabbed at his frozen cheeks. It was snowing. He was colder than snow.

He fell into a soft mound, and understood that he did not have the strength to stand up. He had made a huge mistake in leaving Harth at the base of the mountains. However strong and clever he, Pinguel, might be, he could not cross these freezing mountains by himself.

'Cliffkin,' he whispered. 'Help.'

'Goodnight. Sleep tight,' Cliffkin would say.

The cold was changing to a sort of warmth and comfort.

'Mother,' the boy whispered. 'Help.'

In his longing to be closer to Cliffkin, and to his mother, Pinguel found himself raising his hand to his own neck, without really knowing why. His fingers were numb, yet he could feel their pressure against his skin, and at the same time he imagined something golden and warm in Cliffkin's fingers. Warm. He brought up his other hand too, and in the soft skin between thumb and forefinger he felt a chain.

The Ant Bell. The feel of it brought back Cliffkin's words, all jumbled and confused by the cold.

'If ever, whenever, great danger, wire, ring . . .'

He clutched the bell itself, and tugged until the chain broke. He would hear it ring, anyway, before he died. He brought it to his mouth, felt the wire with his tongue, bit it, and pulled the bell away so that the wire remained between his teeth.

He opened his eyes, and the frigid moonlight showed him his hand and the bell. He raised it high, and waved it back and forth.

It rang loudly, deeply, making a huge sound, as though from a bell a hundred times its size.

He listened to this as it echoed back from the mountains, then brought it close to his chest and fell into unconsciousness.

FORTY ~~~

The ringing soared through gorges and over colourless cliff faces, across The Frozen Wastes, and the Swamplands, all the way to Vizzencourt. Owls and wolves, bears, humans and merryns, wondered at the strange sound. Patrolling Knights of Work galloped into the darkness, on a useless quest for its source, thinking it far nearer than it was. Home in his palace bedroom, Duke Pinchie sat bolt upright, listening most carefully. His face was pale, and his hands began to tremble. Then he jumped from his bed and went to the portrait of the woman, where he stood for some time. He gave a half smile — of relief? of gratitude? it was impossible to say.

Away at the margins of Deep Forest, six blats and attendant hawks woke up and wondered in whispers what the ringing could mean.

Only a single old blat slave, in a barracks on the outskirts of a town not far from Vizzencourt, knew all about it.

To another old blat in the next bunk, he whispered:

'That means that something will happen, soon.'

His friend only sighed, exhausted from a long day spent harvesting olives. His fingertips were stained green from their flesh, and there were still twigs in his hair.

'Cause and effect,' he muttered to himself as he fell asleep.

FORTY-ONE ~~~

Pinguel passed through layers of darkness, each one seeming the darkest anything could be, until he entered the next one. With the cold it was different: he had already travelled through its pain. Now he felt comfortable.

Tangled around the fingers of one outstretched hand was the golden chain of the Ant Bell, the bell itself half-covered by snow.

And now it began to snow more heavily, and as the flakes landed on Pinguel's hands and face, there was no warmth there to melt them. The snow piled up as it does on icy rocks.

A minute or two after Pinguel had stopped breathing, a yellow light, swinging back and forth, appeared in the sky, then another behind it, and a third, and more until this part of the mountainside, from where the ringing of the Ant Bell had come, became entirely honey-coloured.

Wings like those of butterflies, except transparent, sent snow whirling about. An arm wrapped around in cloth that was deep brown in this light, pointed, and the snowy silence was broken by a cry:

'Cristax! Ehue! Menax!'

The lanterns converged on a mound, and a figure knelt and pushed the snow away with a long-fingered, narrow hand that was not human, more like a collection of bendy twigs.

Figures hovered, and others knelt to help with the work until Pinguel was revealed, no longer breathing and now so frozen that, when the first figure picked him up in his arms, his head didn't fall back, nor did his legs bend over the other arm. Snow fell from the boy as the creature made his wings beat faster than before. Surrounded by lantern-carrying comrades, he bore the body of Pinguel high, and higher still up the mountainside, then across a dark valley and up the single highest peak in all the Cold Mountains, where the temperature was even lower than where Pinguel had collapsed.

The Ant Bell slipped from the boy's hand, and glittered in the light from at least thirty lanterns as it fell.

'Staxi!' a figure shouted, and darted to catch it before it had fallen more than two metres.

FORTY-TWO ~~~

Huge and golden, the eyes appeared to have no pupil or iris, so it was hard to know where they were looking.

More like a skull, the face was made of bony stuff with only a glimmer of softness in the muscles around the corners of the mouth. Antennae dangled forward, sensitive to every air current. The neck was made of little panels each about the size of a blat fingernail. The creature wore a shirt or robe made of coarse, brown material, like sackcloth except softer.

Pinguel thought nothing as he stared at the face. He felt no fear, perhaps due to the warmth of the eyes. Besides, he had just woken up, and here was the creature staring down at him. If it wished to harm him it could have done so before now.

'Dia-ah-crattle fix?' asked the creature, tipping its head slightly in a look of concern.

'I don't understand your language. My name is Pinguel.'

The smell of hot bread came to him, and the boy's stomach ached with hunger.

'I . . .' he began.

The creature (the closer Pinguel looked, the more it resembled an ant, a giant ant) took a step back, and with a sort of twitching at the edge of its jaws that might have been a smile, held up a lump of glistening stuff that looked like bread or cake soaked in honey.

And that is what it tasted like, too. The stickiness oozed out as Pinguel bit into it, and some dribbled over the back of his hand. It was the most delicious thing he had ever tasted.

He started to wonder if there would be more, when the ant (if it was an ant) shook its head and held out a blue glass. The drink was sweet, like the bread. Pinguel only had time to make out that he was in a cavern, that he was wearing a robe like that of the ant, that other ants were flying around in the background, and that one wearing a paler robe and carrying a narrow metal staff was flying towards him, before he drifted back to sleep.

FORTY-THREE ～～

The ant with the metal staff briefly held Pinguel's hand, then raised four of his limbs (leaving him standing on just two) and clicked his bony fingers. Three other ants joined him, while six came at a slower speed, carrying a huge slice of bread. Half the ants picked up Pinguel's mattress (another slice of bread) and the six ants placed their slice of bread over Pinguel, and carried him to a steel platform. Joined by hinges, a lid came down, and the two halves pressed the bread tightly around the boy, warming (indeed toasting) it at the same time.

The ant sat before a control panel with a television screen above it that showed Pinguel's skeleton, with the flesh around it blue and orange. When more had turned to orange, and some to red, the ant flicked a switch, and the huge toasting iron yawned open.

FORTY-FOUR ～～

Except for pools of light, some nearby and some further away, in each of which was a bed with a figure beneath a purple blanket, the room was dark.

Pinguel guessed that he was in a hospital. He remembered climbing up the mountain, then lying down. That was all. He reached up to his throat. Something was missing. His neck felt bare. The Ant Bell had gone.

And then he remembered the aching cold, and how he had reached for the bell to ring it.

He felt a tightness in his throat as he recalled the less immediate past: his and Sog's failed quest for Hugo and Peregrine, then Duke Pinchie and the scene at Execution Square.

He had marched straight up the Cold Mountains, and had it not been for the Ant Bell he would now be dead, and the hopes of Cliffkin, Madam and the other blats of Deep Forest dead alongside him. Even Execution Square, he began to think, had been a mistake. What did it matter if he had saved the life of six blats, only to doom all others (and eventually those six, too, when they were recaptured) to slavery under Duke Pinchie and his knights?

He shook his head. 'You are a weak, impulsive, fool,' he told himself. Mercifully, he was tired, and soon fell asleep.

When he awoke, the lights in the infirmary were on and there was a buzz from the wings of at least twenty ants flying in different directions. On a chair next to Pinguel's bed sat the ant with the staff and light blue robe who had visited the boy the previous evening.

He leaned closer.

'I do not speak your language well.' His voice was like the click-clack of knitting needles. 'I taught myself from a book, and have never spoken to such as you. You are understanding me, perhaps?'

'I am, yes.'

Something like a smile tweaked at the ant's jaw muscles. Momentarily, it lowered its antennae. 'Our illustrious Queen sends you her regards, most first of all. I am her Prime Minister. My name is Tixtl.'

'Mine is Pinguel.'

'You are the possessor of the Ant Bell, so are a most honoured guest. We had to cook you severely. You were almost blue.'

'The Ant Bell,' Pinguel found himself asking. 'It's so small. How did you hear it through the snow?'

'We have splendid hearing. Especially for that bell. Many years ago, a member of our royal family, on a mission of discovery, found himself attacked by winged creatures. Badly injured, he sought refuge in a forest, and this was granted him by a creature known as a blat. You are such a one, unless I am mistaken.'

'Yes,' acknowledged Pinguel.

'He returned at another time, inside a welcoming blizzard, and presented the blat with a bell, to allow us to return the favour, which now we have so done, to our great pleasure.'

'Can you take me down to the other side of these mountains? But my clothes, and boots . . .'

'Warmed most nicely. You will be well enough to leave after one more sleep. The marrow at the centre of your bones froze. Your heart became solid ice. We were uncertain that we would have the power to revive you. You are strong, blat Pinguel.'

'Do you know where I can find Hugo, the famous human, or Peregrine the Wizard?'

The ant shook his head. 'No, but I can tell you that at the base of the mountains is a large building, and that not far away, in the waters off the coast, lies a vessel inhabited by, among others, a creature larger than a thousand Tixtls, and capable of even quicker flight.'

'That might be Hugo's boat,' Pinguel murmured.

The ant watched carefully. After a short silence, he commented:

'We are much in admiration of your strength, but we cannot share your interest in the world beyond these mountains, or temples, as they are to us. Here we have our tunnels and passages. We grow our food beneath electric lights, and fertilise the soil with chemicals perfected by our scientists. The Lower World is for us,' he paused, calmly selecting words, 'a realm of indifference. I am to inform you that you may remain here, if you wish, where there will always be food and warmth for you. You will have a chamber of your own, and the means wherewith to study. If you leave and come back, you will always be our honoured guest. Our Queen does not receive visitors; she takes even less interest in Below than the rest of us. Please think, and tell me your decision upon waking from your next sleep.'

Pinguel struggled to get out of bed, but a new attack of gloom at having failed to climb the Cold Mountains, combined with doubts about the future, caused him to fall asleep again. When he awoke, the blue-robed ant was again beside his bed.

'I would like to go down to the hall and the boat,' he said. 'Thank you for your invitation, but I can't stay here.'

With its purple blankets in pools of light, the room was beautiful. In two other beds were ants, attended now and then by nurses. The rest were empty. A sudden longing kept Pinguel motionless, as when he had been frozen on the mountainside. He craved to belong to this world, to some world, to a place where he could be at the centre instead of always on the outside and different to others. To belong, to *belong*. What must it feel like?

His clothes had been cleaned and pressed, his canvas shoes rubbed with a resinous stuff to make them waterproof. Running his fingers through his black, shoulder-length hair, expecting to find tangles, its softness told him that the ants had washed and brushed it as he slept.

Once again he was tempted to remain here, in ignorance of the world. Finally he forced himself to stand up.

Tixtl presented the boy with a blue robe, like his own.

'Folds up to be capable of fitting into a small space,' he explained. 'Necessary if you wish to endure external cold. I feel that I will see you again, some day, and confess that despite my indifference to the world outside, I look forward to that hour.'

Brown-robed ants joined them. One picked up Pinguel and held him in his arms. Between the infirmary and the mountain's outer exit were five other doors, opened by automatic machinery as the ants approached. Beyond each, the air was colder. Pinguel tucked his hands beneath the robe, and brought the cowl up around his face, leaving only his eyes and forehead exposed.

With the opening of the final door, into a world that with its dazzle of light after the caves appeared to be wholly white, the cold stung Pinguel's face so acutely that if it hadn't been for his eagerness to see what lay beyond the Cold Mountains he would have pulled the robe right over his head.

They were in a blizzard. The ants angled their flight into gusts, like ships tacking through a storm. Then suddenly the sky cleared, and Pinguel glimpsed a line of blue in the distance. They descended through more cloud and snow and the blue returned as a duller shade near a mass of dark rock at the base of the mountains. Huge waves crashed onto these, making a noise like a storm's wind in the trees of Deep Forest. Further down was a tall building with towers at each corner, made of dark, mountain stone. Pinguel's ears felt blocked. He shouted goodbye to the ants, who had deposited him beside a path just above the hall, but they had caught a gust of wind and were already whirling to join the distance.

FORTY-FIVE ~~~

Near the horizon floated a ship many times the size of the hall, and sure enough, in the sky above, a creature far larger than an elephant was flying. Its long tail swayed, like a flexible rudder, and its wings blurred like those of a hummingbird.

Tufts of straw-coloured grass grew alongside the path and between rocks, but no trees or bushes relieved the bareness. Even on the plain before Vizzencourt, or in The Frozen Wastes, Pinguel had never felt so much in the open.

Either side of the hall's main double door stood a wooden packing case, labelled FRAGILE. Everything was human-sized; each step to the door came to Pinguel's shoulders, and the packing cases were five blat-storeys high.

One half of the double doors stood open. With each step, the boy climbed into greater silence. His legs were weak from his freezing and days in bed. Everything now depended on him. He felt terribly alone, and yet . . .

As he entered the hall, the sea noises hushed to a murmur. More packing cases, boxes, suitcases, briefcases, hatboxes and luggage of every sort lay around the walls. Most were human-sized or larger, but there were blat-scale satchels, too, that reminded him of school, as well as wicker picnic baskets, backpacks, and drawstring bags in a heap at the foot of yet another crate marked FRAGILE.

At the end of the hall, another set of double doors opened onto darkness. Pinguel peered inside, and made out the huge tyres, then the rest of an enormous semi-trailer in shadow.

'Hello, Your Highness,' came a small voice from somewhere in the hall of luggage.

Pinguel swung around, but saw nothing.

'Your Highness! Your Highness!' came further voices, seemingly out of nowhere.

PART SEVEN

A packing case trembled, a corner fell away (without any splintering noise), then the top folded, a corner became rounded, darker colours appeared, and before Pinguel could jump back or be alarmed, a bear in blue overalls was standing before him, wiping paws on a yellow rag and growling as he bowed, 'Greetings, Your Highness.'

Everything was moving. Luggage rolled over, straightened, changed its form. Satchels unfolded their flaps, spun shoulder-straps, and twisted buckles until they became belts holding up the baggy, brown trousers of a pair of strange-looking creatures who were blat-sized, yet whose noses, like Pinguel's, were too short to belong to blats. (Nor did they have the shortish legs and arms of merryns.) One had a golden ring through his nose, and the other had spindly arms and legs, hardly a muscle on them, and wore a metal neck brace to support a head too large for his body.

'Greetings, Your Highness. My name is Ring,' spoke the one with a ring through his nose, bowing. His arm, though, went to the back of his friend, to support him.

'And mine is Genius.' The large-headed one spoke in a softer voice. 'Greetings, King Opthalomicus.'

Genius's hair was pale orange, and his eyes had so little colour in them it was hard to say what colour, exactly, they were.

Crates, boxes and suitcases continued to transform themselves. As each creature ceased to be a piece of luggage, it bowed and said, 'Hail, King Opthalomicus!' Two adult humans transformed themselves from a single packing case, the woman holding a baby with a blue bonnet and matching mittens. The man (once he had bowed to Pinguel) brought a rattle from his pocket and waved it before the infant's face.

'There we are. See? Don't cry. We aren't luggage any more. And here's the king we've been waiting for.'

Bears and wolves were bowing and waving, but only one other creature, apart from Ring and Genius, turned out to be of Pinguel's size.

He began as a small parcel of brown paper and string, with black letters across it in a language Pinguel had never seen.

The string unknotted to form the border of a short, brown cape, and the paper whirled to fill in the rest of this garment. An arm appeared within a bright red sleeve, then came two black boots. A belt whipped between a white shirt and black trousers, but the strangest thing of all was the creature's skin. It was pale blue. As the creature opened his mouth, Pinguel was reassured to notice that his tongue was pink.

'Greetings, Highness.' Voice dry, like river pebbles grating together.

Ring touched his shoulder. 'Allow me to introduce Ouk.'

Ouk nodded. 'I am Peregrine's assistant. Yes, Peregrine the Wizard. We expect him soon.'

Pinguel remembered the story that Sog had told on the road outside Vizzencourt, of a wizard treading on a sharp stone, and finding a friend.

Ouk continued:

'We are your subjects, King Opthalomicus of the Titans. We have been waiting for this day for —'

'Ages,' supplied Ring.

'For two hundred and eighteen years, five months, one week, two days, four hours, six minutes, and two seconds,' supplied Genius.

'I hope you aren't fond of rules,' Ring muttered with a look of such intensity that Pinguel took half a step back, while also feeling attracted to this strange creature.

'I'm not a king,' he found himself murmuring. 'Is this a joke?' He felt faint — all this strangeness made him dizzy. He staggered, and would have fallen but for the nose of an old wolf nudging him in the small of his back.

'Good!' shouted Ring. 'You don't seem bossy anyway. Let's eat then. To the truck!'

FORTY-SEVEN ~~~

The dark inside of the semi-trailer flickered with small electric lights that showed a long table crowded with dishes, and smelling so delicious to Pinguel that, once again, he felt faint. For Ouk and the titans there were stairs up to the table, and a red carpet all the way down, between bowls of food, to four chairs at the end. Everyone else sat on backless benches.

Behind the small chairs a door opened, and humans wearing white aprons bustled out carrying steaming dishes.

'It'll get cold,' muttered one of these, 'if you don't start eating straightaway.'

'Before we start!' Ouk stood up, removed his cloak, and held up a hand for silence.

'Before we start, allow me to welcome King Opthalomicus on behalf of all of us, and particularly on behalf of Peregrine the Wizard, the founder of the Order of Stowaways, of which we are all members, and who

I know would be here if he could. I also happen to know that Hugo the Dancer, Timberwell the Dragon, and the blats and humans aboard the *SS Orestea* also send you their best wishes. They would be here, were it not necessary for them to care for their ship.'

'Enough speech,' whispered Ring.

A smaller table was placed before the titans and Ouk, then dishes of rissoles, and fried potato slices with a sauce that reminded Pinguel of his meals at Madam's house.

'You will wish to ask questions,' began Genius, seated on the other side of Ouk.

'Eat first,' Ring advised. 'As one of your two royal advisers, that is what I advise.'

Ouk was the only one not eating. Even Genius raised a long-handled spoon all the way to his mouth (the neck brace making it impossible to bend his head) and took a sip of clear soup.

'Peregrine drew us your portrait,' Ouk told Pinguel. 'He knew you would come, even knew the time to the nearest week. So we have been waiting.'

'But a *king*,' Pinguel whispered back, voice not carrying past the little table because of all the eating noises made by wolves, bears and humans, and by the cries of the human baby.

'Yes, king. I should warn you, there isn't any doubt about it,' Genius confirmed. 'And what is "Opthalomicus"? Our world, the world of titans. And you can't abdicate because you don't have a brother, sister, son or daughter to inherit the title. It's clearly stated in Chapter 17 —'

'Of the Book of Boredom,' cut in Ring, nose-ring twinkling. 'The good news is that we're in for mayhem.

A *king*,' he emphasised, mockery gone from his voice. 'We titans have been searching for you for a long time. Half of us are more or less uncontrollable. Left alone, we would wreck so-called civilisation for the sheer fun of doing so. The other half ... well, you've met your uncle. Duke Pinchie.'

'My uncle!'

'Your father's brother, Highness,' put in Genius.

A wolf raised a glass of wine to King Opthalomicus's table, and splashed some over the arm of the bear beside him. If it hadn't been for the presence of the king, this might have caused an argument.

Meanwhile (as Ring drank and ate as greedily as any wolf), Genius took over the explaining. 'Duke Pinchie overthrew your real father, the previous king. Your mother fled into the forest, to seek refuge with the blats' famous magicians. In those days, in this part of the world, the Order of Stowaways did not exist.'

Genius had lowered his voice. Pinguel had to lean closer to hear, pulling the ants' blue robe closer against a chill in the air.

'Your father,' went on Genius, 'died in the duke's dungeons, your mother in Deep Forest, as you probably know, at the paws of savage' — he lowered his voice even further — 'wolves. But that was their way, remember. Hunger is impatient, and food is scarce.

'You are a member of the Hendersonian branch of titans, to which your father belonged, and of the Mayhem line. Ring here —'

'Is your other uncle, of the Mayhem line,' supplied this titan, hair sticking up more proudly than ever. 'Your mother's younger brother.'

In the lamplit seconds before either Genius or Ring resumed, Pinguel experienced a sense of power that grew from his fingertips and travelled towards his heart. Despite the strange blend of emotions that he now felt, hearing of his parents, he knew that he was, truly and for the first time, slipping into a place where he belonged. This came not so much as a surprise as a relief.

Yet whatever else he might be, Pinguel's upbringing had made him a blat. His real father and mother were dead; there was nothing he could do about that. He had never known them. But perhaps he could help the blats.

'We must rescue them,' he found himself saying. 'And there are others in Deep Forest to be saved. And' — he raised his voice so that not only the titans and Ouk at his table could hear, but also the facing rows of wolves, bears and humans beyond. 'And there are wolves to be saved too. My best friend is a wolf: Graf, an artist. Thank you for your welcome, everyone. Thank you, for making me feel so much at home.'

Pinguel didn't hear Genius whisper to Ring:

'Hear that? Didn't I tell you: a born king,' and Ring's answer:

'Yes, proposes reckless action, straightaway.'

FORTY-EIGHT ~~~

'Tomorrow you will begin learning to be luggage, my Lord,' murmured Ouk as he unrolled a sleeping bag in a corner of the vast (to a titan), carpeted shelf behind the truck driver's seat.

The feast was continuing in the rear trailer, and would do so for the rest of the night. Genius, Ouk and Pinguel had left early because there was so much work to be done tomorrow.

'You will pick it up quickly,' Ouk assured the boy-king as he brushed a strand of hair away from his pale blue face. 'The wolves are the hardest to teach, together with the titans of the Mayhem line. Impatience is the greatest obstacle to successful impersonation of luggage.'

'You have come so far,' soothed Genius as he pulled his sleeping bag up around his neck brace and stretched out beside the boy-king. 'You have been well cared for by the ants, but you need more time to rest.'

The cab became dark as Ouk turned out a lamp.

'Peregrine should be here,' he muttered. 'It would be useful to have him, but he has been delayed before.'

'Where is he?' wondered Pinguel, who longed to meet the famous wizard.

'Some say he is a prisoner among the Tortured Isles, beyond the Winedark Sea. Tinderwell, the dragon — you might have glimpsed him flying over the ship as you came down the mountain path today — has a different theory. He believes there is a possibility that Peregrine has found a cottage, and is sitting in a deep armchair with his feet on the windowsill, watching changes in the weather and reading books. It is his one weakness: a tendency to contemplation. But I don't know ...'

'Now we must sleep,' put in Genius. 'Goodnight, Your Highness.'

The mechanism in the brilliant titan's neck brace creaked as he eased his head onto a pillow.

The double metal walls (the cabin of the truck, then the container beyond) blocked all but the loudest feasting noises. Ring was racing a circuit of the table, using the guests' heads as stepping stones, while holding a full tumbler (human-sized) of red wine, a difficult balancing task even for a titan. He ended up splashing it over the snout of a brown bear. The animal gave a bellow of rage and swatted the titan, claws retracted, into a tomato salad, where Ring lay awhile, exhausted, a smile across his mayhem-loving face.

But these noises were not the cause of Pinguel's sleeplessness. As Ouk and Genius dreamed beside him, King Opthalomicus thought of his mother seeking refuge in Deep Forest and meeting only savage wolves, and of his father, killed by his own brother, Pinchie, whom Pinguel had met so briefly, as though in the depths of a dream. He thought of Breathing Taxes, executions and Blat Magic, and tried to think up a plan; but for some strange reason (he could not say why, no matter how hard he thought) he remembered, and then could not stop thinking about (until these thoughts became dreams), a particular night, one on which a boy had peered through the window of his father's study to see a tiny girl licking syrup from the tips of her fingers.

FORTY-NINE ~~~

The next morning everyone breakfasted in the truck, where the only signs of last night's mayhem were glistenings of red wine in the cracks where floor met wall. The human cleaners had given it a quick mopping; later they would hose it out.

Before Pinguel could take a bite of his toast and honey a deep hoot came from outside.

'That will be the *Orestea*,' Genius remarked.

Ring put his hands over his ears. 'They should not make such a noise on the morning after a feast.'

'The *Orestea*,' resumed Genius, 'is our means of escape. Ways through the mountains exist, but far from here, so it will not be long before Pinchie's aeroplanes find us, and his knights will follow quickly. We would be outnumbered but, more importantly, like blats, we have little stomach for pitched battles and their chancey outcomes.'

The breeze stirred Genius's thin, ginger hair as he talked. As though focused on the riches of intelligence and reasoning within, rather than on the slightly less fascinating world outside, his eyes were closed.

'Some of us,' put in Ring, 'would disagree with that. If the enemy want to fight, then sooner or later, in my experience, you find yourself backed in a corner, and then it's either give battle or give up.'

'Oh no,' protested Ouk. 'Have I told you how Peregrine answers that argument? You can always change yourself into a fierce-looking monster, and scare your foe away, or you can make them laugh, or —'

'Or,' interrupted Genius, 'you can do as Hugo did, on a famous occasion not so long ago. Faced with a hoard of fight-hungry hunters, he performed a dance that so entranced them he was able to rescue Toskin the blat, now one of the *Orestea*'s two chief explorers.'

'All very well for some people,' muttered Ring, 'but —'

'And now,' Ouk interrupted, 'I think it is time for your first luggage lesson, Your Highness.'

Ring helped Genius down the stairs from the table. Although Ring disagreed with almost everything the wise titan said, he was always on the lookout for ways to assist him.

The human cleaners were filling buckets from taps near the back door of the truck. The hall itself was deserted except for a small pile of rubbish in a corner, mainly composed of string and brown paper.

Ouk, Ring, Genius and Pinguel halted, the boy pulling the blue ant robe tighter around his shoulders. There was a chilly draught in the room.

Just as he realised that everyone was looking at him, a voice came from he couldn't tell exactly where:

'Tell me, what was life like among the ants? I've always been fascinated by the ants of the Cold Mountains.'

Ring laughed at the puzzled expression on Pinguel's face, then closed his eyes as he remembered his headache. Ouk was grinning, cape tossed carelessly back over one shoulder. Even Genius's eyes were open and twinkling with amusement.

They were waiting, Pinguel realised, to see what he would do. Was this some sort of test?

'Life among the ants,' he replied, having no idea whom he was addressing, 'was peaceful. They brought me to life by placing me between slices of toasting bread. By the way, which of you is a ventriloquist?'

Pinguel turned to Ring, because it was just the sort of trick he would play. But the titan shook his head.

Then the mysterious voice returned: thin, fragile, making Pinguel think of a dried-out twig:

'No one here is a ventriloquist, Your Highness. I visited the ants myself, many years ago. They were kind to me. I too had become frozen. If only they would take a greater interest in the world, they would be a great force for good.'

Pinguel was thinking hard. The voice belonged to none of the three before him, he was certain. So someone was invisible, nearby, or . . .

The pile of rubbish.

Made up of string, bits of paper, and one or two dust balls at its base. The draught stirred an edge of the paper.

Something strange about this pile of rubbish.

Pinguel's mind worked quickly, even for a titan.

'I know,' he said aloud, this time addressing the rubbish. 'You're a highly advanced sort of rubbish. Not too tidy, not too chaotic. So by being not quite perfect, you are *absolutely* perfect.'

As Genius murmured, 'Well done', and Ring and Ouk also nodded approval, the rubbish began to stir.

It reminded Pinguel of a television film he had once seen of an explosion in reverse. Instead of being blasted outwards, the earth, wood and other material was sucked rapidly in, giving last of all a shiver of adjustment as each bit fitted precisely back where it belonged. This is what happened to the pile of rubbish, and at the end of it a blat-sized figure, wearing a brown robe with a hood at the back and knotted around with a rope at the waist, and with white hair, a long, blattish nose, pale blue eyes, and shoulders bent over a walking stick with a duck's head carved out of green alabaster for the handle, was smiling before him.

'Allow me to introduce Zoffani,' began Ouk in a low, respectful voice, 'who, with Peregrine the Wizard, was the original founder of the Order of Stowaways.'

The blat-monk gave a low bow.

'An honour to meet you, King Opthalomicus. Having been brought up with blats, you will appreciate the closeness of our ideals to those of the Stowaways. To become luggage, really, is little more than a combination of blat disappearing skills with portability.'

'To become a pile of rubbish,' put in Genius with an admiring glance at the monk, 'one must learn and practise for many years.'

Zoffani made a dismissive gesture merely by raising his fingers off the duck's head, as though to say, 'It's nothing, really.'

'Now, Your Highness.' He surveyed Pinguel from the boy's cloth and rubber blat-shoes and green trousers, to his jacket knitted by Madam, long black hair, blue ant-robe ...

'You I see as a slender, newish briefcase, one likely to contain important documents which will turn out, however, to be in an ancient, indecipherable language. Shall we begin our training?'

All Zoffani gave Pinguel to help him become a briefcase was a single sheet of folded leather, frayed at the corners, and an old handle that had once belonged to a real briefcase. Zoffani taught the boy to fold the leather, and to position both the handle and his limbs so as to allow him to remain comfortable for long periods, and even to read a book or watch TV (using a tiny set and headphones).

When they had practised for some time, the old monk lectured Pinguel on the essential trick of becoming luggage.

'Concentrate your attention on the handle,' he advised. 'It is by far the most important part. And here comes the surprise: the angle of the handle must be a little *unnatural*. Just as you observed that, when I was being rubbish, the string was too tight near the lower edge. This detail will distract even the most suspicious enemy, and discourage them from closer examination of the whole.'

As Zoffani spoke, Pinguel was reminded of those long winter afternoons when he and the rest of his class had been lectured by Boboscular on the skills of remaining silent. How had such skills helped the blats, when their forest had been invaded by Lord Pinchie's Knights of Work?

Pinguel could not forget his surprise and then despair at being unable to cross the Cold Mountains.

Obviously, like the blats, he could not do *anything* that he wished. Perhaps there was not much, after all, that he *could* do.

He had sunk into coldness and sleep in the snow, and now found himself remembering this with fondness.

'You are not concentrating, Your Highness,' Zoffani corrected. 'The handle, you will observe —'

But he was interrupted by the yelp of a wolf from outside the main door. 'Attention! Assume your posts! A stranger, in the South Passage! Estimated time of arrival: two minutes and ten seconds.'

FIFTY ~~~

'We prefer to be luggage when strangers arrive,' Ouk explained as he began, by pulling his cape out wide, to turn himself into a tiny sack of river gravel. 'It allows us to observe them, and if they are hostile we have the element of surprise.'

'Your handle is not tilting quite far enough back,' pointed out Zoffani, more than halfway turned into a pile of rubbish.

Showing no sign of panic or haste, bears and wolves were transforming themselves into crates, trunks and suitcases. Ring produced a piece of grey material from his pocket, and with the help of a grimy length of string became a sack that looked as if it contained the castors for a chair: something too useful to throw out but hardly worth investigating. But it was Genius who most surprised Pinguel. From beneath his neck brace he pulled a light, silky-grey cloth down to his feet, then (having trodden on the edges to keep it there) over his head. Beneath it, he extruded wires, and when he had finished adjusting these it was just as though, there by the wall, was a block of concrete that someone had put aside and forgotten about.

The hall became so deeply and calmly silent that no one could possibly suspect, in the midst of it, that they were far from alone.

Pinguel's arm ached from holding up the handle.

Then he heard small, light footsteps.

They sounded tired. After the shoe touched the floor, there was a sad, whispery noise as the toe scraped along. Pinguel's eyes stung from staring. He blinked, and straight afterwards saw, at the centre of the hall, a small, terribly thin, bent-over figure, with shoulder-length white hair and a pointed blat nose.

He thought he knew who it was, but was only certain when the blat spoke, saying:

'What I wouldn't give,' he sighed, 'for a mint julep. Even for one with no mint, and no julep, I'd pay all the money I have.'

Pinguel listened hard; there seemed to be no one else present. As Ring, beside him, stirred, and all the luggage began to tremble, he called out:

'Sarin! Sarin!'

'Why' — cried the old Far Scout — 'it's Pinguel.'

'King Opthalomicus to you!' growled Ring, pushing the grey cloth back into his pocket.

'King!' Although Sarin's eyes were round with wonder, there was still a trace of amusement in their wrinkled-up corners. 'Haven't *you* done well for yourself!'

He took another step towards Pinguel, then stumbled, and — the crinkled look of amusement never leaving his eyes — muttered 'mint julep' as he sank unconscious to the floor.

They carried him to the cushioned front seat of the truck, and a human chef brought along a small (for a human, large for a blat) glass of mint julep.

The smell alone was enough to cause the old Far Scout to open his eyes and sit up. He reached out both hands, and drank off the emerald green mixture, mint leaf and ice floating on top, in one go.

'Thank you,' he muttered, staring longingly at the empty glass.

'Another one, please,' Genius asked the human.

With the tip of a finger, Sarin caught a droplet at the corner of his mouth, and licked it up.

'So I have reached the coast, and the rumours are true, and better...' He closed his eyes and took a deep breath. Some of the tiny veins across his eyelids were red, others blue-green. When he raised them, Pinguel asked, thinking of his own failed attempt to cross the Cold Mountains:

'But how did you get here?'

The next mint julep arrived, and now the old blat sat up straight, strength fully restored.

'Yes, yes, I'll bring another,' the human sighed.

'Polite, aren't they?' Sarin nodded in the direction of what, to him, was a departing giant. 'I had thought they would be rougher, from their TV programs. Certainly I did not expect to see them taking orders from a blat or...' He glanced, uncertain, from Ring and Genius to Pinguel. 'Well, you aren't merryns. Your legs aren't short enough.'

'We're titans,' Pinguel answered. 'But how did you get here? What news do you have of the blats?'

Having drunk his third mint julep, the Far Scout was ready for anything.

'I followed the edge of Dragon's Tooth, then took a trail that I knew from the old days. I deceived the mountains into thinking that I was heading straight for them, and you should have seen the blizzard they created to prevent me! But my trick worked: they froze the River Quispiam, so I ducked behind a waterfall and into a network of tunnels and crevices that — perhaps I flatter myself, but I don't think so — only a Far Scout of at least fifty years' training could follow. I arrived far down the coast, where the marshes and swamps go all the way to the sea. Luckily I found some lotus flowers there. I crushed their petals over my arms and neck to keep away the mosquitos.

'News? Only that the days of blats in Deep Forest are over. Over! Knights of Work covered the trees in fine-meshed nets, then cut down some of them, burned others, and took hostages of the first blats they captured.

'I swear I heard those old trees cry out in pain. Used

to gentle treatment, to cradling blats, the knights came as a frightful shock. Many leaves turned white from fear and disappointment, before even a whisper of fire touched them. My home was outside the net, and even with my far-scouting skills there was nothing I could do to help the blats or trees. So I made my way here, to the coast, to seek help.'

'And help you shall have,' Pinguel found himself vowing, his anger growing as the flames and smoke had done in Deep Forest.

He went to the door of the truck and called to a group of humans standing around near the back wheels:

'Do you have any syrup suitable for putting on pancakes?'

'Yes, Your Highness.'

'We'll need a bottle of it, please.'

He turned back into the truck, and caught Genius's eye.

'Yes, you *are* our king.' The brilliant titan spoke softly. 'And as your adviser, can I tell you that I agree with you? The time for action has indeed arrived.'

Ring gave a jump of excitement, and clapped Ouk on the back.

'But what is wrong?' Genius asked, as Pinguel raised a hand to his eyes.

'I...' the boy began.

'Go on,' Sarin encouraged.

'I have made stupid decisions in the past,' Pinguel continued in a softer voice. 'Now I *doubt —*'

'No!' Ring and Ouk began to protest, but Genius, by simply holding out his hands in a calming gesture, and speaking in his soft voice, cut them off.

'No, there must be a decision,' he began. 'And to do nothing is itself a decision.' He gave a smile, and nodded so that his neck brace gave a little squeak. 'And *all* decisions have uncertain consequences. Luck is always necessary for success. And we trust your luck, King Opthalomicus. So tell us, what have you decided?'

FIFTY-ONE ~~~

'The forest first,' began Pinguel once again, doubts forgotten, all in a rush. 'Oh, thank you.'

He took a blat-sized bottle of syrup from between a human finger and thumb.

'We go to the forest. But how?' He turned to Sarin. 'You spoke of a narrow path, and swamp. This truck —'

'Tinderwell, the dragon, can help with that...' murmured Genius.

As they made their plans, the king couldn't help seeing what they were risking: not only the lives of many creatures, but also the whole cause of non-Hendersonian civilisation.

Everyone would go — it was decided — except for Ouk and Zoffani, who would wait behind for Peregrine. A human radioed the ship, and as soon as it was dark a fluttery humming (not unlike that of the propellors of huge, old-fashioned aircraft, but minus the motor sound) grew louder over the hall.

The truck motor roared, and two bears threw open the garage doors. The night was cold. Pinguel, Genius and Ring sat in armchairs bolted to the dashboard, while a bear gently prodded the accelerator and peered into his side-mirror to make sure they were clear of the building.

They had driven over, and stopped in the middle of, an X-pattern of chains which the humans, being the best climbers of all the creatures present (although the bears would have disputed this if anyone had dared say it to their faces), now attached to a cable over the middle of the huge truck. They clattered and stomped on the roof, with all but the occasional shouted word drowned by the throbbing of wings. Leaning forward, Pinguel glimpsed the pale underside of the dragon's chin and neck, about twenty metres above. Tinderwell looked to be a little narrower than the truck, but quite a bit longer. Although his wings were beating so fast that they were visible only as blurs, his body, like that of a hummingbird reaching with its beak for the nectar at the centre of a flower, remained perfectly still.

With the chains fastened to the cable, which had a loop at one end to go around the dragon's neck, the bear driver (whose name was Orsus) pulled back the handbrake and snapped on his seatbelt.

'We'd better do the same,' warned Genius. 'I've done this before. The truck tilts sharply when Tinderwell picks it up.'

'It's more fun inside the back,' Ring mentioned with a faraway look. 'Everyone slides to the doors, which have been lined with mattresses.'

'What about weapons?' Pinguel wondered. 'What do we have in the truck?'

'Nothing much,' Ring answered. 'Cannons, machine guns, atomic bombs ... but the white-heat flamethrower is the best.'

'No,' sighed Genius. 'Only a few spears, and bows and arrows, if we remembered to bring them. We could never hope to defeat the Hendersonians in a war. If we gain a victory, it will be due to a blend of daring, timidity, planning and accidents.'

'With perhaps the tiniest bit of fighting thrown in,' Ring had to add.

'That is, of course, if Your Highness ... But wait!'

They braced themselves as the chain rattled and the truck jerked up, front first. They teetered, as though the chains had come loose and were about to fall, before being lifted strongly and confidently into the night air.

With his back pressed into the armchair, and looking up, Pinguel had a much better view of the underside of the dragon. Parallel across his neck and stomach were faint grey lines. His short front legs were neatly tucked up and his paws folded under.

Ring hopped to the passenger window and leaned out to adjust the side mirror.

'To see the ground,' he explained as Tinderwell continued to gain altitude, still following the coast, before crossing the Cold Mountains.

'Are there other dragons?' Pinguel asked Genius, thinking how useful they would be in any conflict with the duke's forces.

'We believe so, but only as far away as the Pelagian Islands, or beyond. There are certainly stories of them being there. Ouk suspects that Peregrine may be on his way back from that area, perhaps with — who knows? — hundreds of them.'

Now Tinderwell wheeled, and Ring jumped to the bar that held the mirror to the door. Back in his armchair, with the mirror at the correct angle and the window rolled up, he pulled a scarf from his jacket pocket.

'It's going to get very cold,' he warned.

Pinguel pulled up the collar of his jacket, and wrapped the Ant Robe closer around him. He had become attached to this; it reminded him of the ant infirmary and its purple blankets, and gave him a feeling of safety. Last night he had woken to find himself rubbing it between a forefinger and thumb, next to his cheek.

Although the windows were shut and air vents closed, the cabin of the truck chilled quickly as they approached the summit of the Cold Mountains. Snow whirled at them, and ice crystals appeared on the windscreen.

'Mountains didn't have time,' grunted Orsus in his gruff, bear's voice, 'to prepare proper welcome.'

This chimed with something Pinguel remembered hearing from Sarin, but had been too busy to question: about the mountains making snow and extra cold to halt his climb.

'Do they really ...?' he began, turning to Genius, who, in his brilliance, had anticipated what the boy was going to say:

'Many believe that the mountains can sense an approaching intruder and, because of their pride at being the highest and coldest in the world, do their best to freeze them to death or, at least, to make them turn back.'

'But do you think —?'

'In the country where I come from, near my old school, there was a hill that would do its best to trip up anyone who dared to run down it. But —'

'Shsh!' Ring commanded, pointing into the night sky. 'Action!'

With a noise like a blade being whisked across stone, an arrow shape, gleaming in starlight, was coming straight for them.

'What? Where?' demanded Orsus, whose eyesight was not as good as that of the titans.

'A jet aeroplane,' Genius answered in a voice that sounded oddly calm. 'And we have only one defence against such an attack.'

'But a good defence! Oh, what a *good* defence it is!' shouted Ring, hopping up and down on his seat. 'A most excellent defence!'

Before Pinguel could ask what this was, the truck veered as Tinderwell faced the jet. Then two objects like sharks, except with fins below as well as above, fell from the plane, spurted out white stuff from behind, and proceeded to race one another, even faster than the jet, towards them.

'Missiles,' sighed Ring.

Pinguel barely had time to wonder how anyone could be so happy at the probability of being blown up, and Genius just had time to say 'Hold on!' when a long jet of flame, deep red at its core, poured from above them towards the missiles and jet.

The engulfed missiles exploded immediately, and the force of the dragon's flames whipped back these blasts towards the jet.

Just before the aircraft entered this angry cloud of fire, a white object flew up from behind its pointed nose, and opened into a tranquil umbrella that just managed to avoid the flames.

A second later the aircraft exploded, and Tinderwell had to lose altitude quickly to duck underneath.

'A *most* excellent defence,' sighed Ring, eyes still full of the explosion.

'Tinderwell will be exhausted,' put in Genius. 'Dragons use a lot of energy, doing that. He'll have to put us down quite near the Cold Mountains, and soon the whole of Pinchie's airforce will be here.'

FIFTY-TWO ~~~

The truck came to rest with a series of jolts that its double-pneumatic suspension turned into springy little jumps. When the humans had unfastened the chains, Tinderwell brought his face close to the windscreen.

'Greetings, King Opthalomicus of the Titans,' he said in a deep voice. His huge eyes were green around their pupils, golden on the outside. 'Hugo sends his greetings, as do Nadia, Septimus, Humfel, Mintra, Grofway, Cumber, Romfy, Toskin, Janice, and everyone else aboard the *Orestea*. You know how to contact me. I hope to see you soon.'

The humans outside the truck bowed low, hands over their ears to protect themselves from the fierce draught of the dragon's wings.

Orsus turned on powerful headlights, started the motor, and when two thumps at the back of the cab indicated that the humans had bundled themselves and the chains back inside, they began to move along a gravel road at the border of The Frozen Wastes and the Swamplands.

The road went in a straight line. Soon the noise of the truck's motor was drowned by the shriek of jets.

'Shouldn't we turn off the headlights?' Pinguel wondered.

Orsus shook his head. 'Others drive here, Highness. They are not sure that we are the ones that flew.'

And sure enough, within minutes other headlights blinked around a bend, and a bear driver honked his horn in greeting to a fellow late-night trucker.

It wasn't long before they came to their first roadblock. Knights stood across the road in two groups of ten beside a row of their armoured horses.

'In the old days,' Ring murmured to himself, 'we'd have burst through, and with any luck one of the knights would have jumped on the back, climbed to the roof, and I would have to go out to wrestle with him.

'Nowadays,' he groaned as he unbuckled his seatbelt, 'we hide under the dashboard.'

As the truck slowed, the titans (with Ring as usual tenderly assisting Genius) climbed among red- and green-coloured wires, like vines in a dense forest, and heard the booming voice of a Knight of Work as the truck halted.

'Open up the back! We're looking for fugitives!'

The other knights clanked around, the sharp edges of their swords twinkling in starlight.

'I gotta schedule to keep,' grumbled the bear as he opened the door, letting in a blast of cold that made the three titans shiver. Pinguel took off his blue robe, and wrapped it around Genius. Being here among the wires was not unlike wintry hiding practice in Deep Forest.

The knights clanked away with Orsus, and the titans heard the heavy back doors being unlatched and thrown open.

'When the knights see what's inside,' whispered Ring, 'they will come close to collapsing from boredom. Surrounded by such a typical, dusty cargo, such ordinary and believable luggage, they'll have to get out as quickly as they can to breathe fresh air.'

They were stopped twice more by roadblocks of Knights of Work before they reached Deep Forest, or what had once gone by that name.

FIFTY-THREE ⌇⌇

It was the bleakest of a day's twenty-four hours (with perhaps the exception of between three and four on a grey Sunday afternoon). The hour before dawn, with frail light filtering through clouds. Bulldozers and trucks, graders and levellers, appeared beside the road, next to rows of tents for drivers and mechanics. Wisps of smoke and charcoal, the remnants of week-old fires, hung in the air. Past the heavy equipment were pyramid-shaped stacks of huge logs, with rougher branches in between.

The sight of all these logs, lying so silently, gave Pinguel a sense of coldness almost as deep as the snow and ice of Cold Mountains. They drove past more logs and equipment until they came to a pyramid-shaped sign that spanned the road.

'Slow down,' whispered Genius to the bear. 'Let's see what it says.'

Orsus changed gear, and switched the headlights onto high beam:

DUKE PINCHIE MEMORIAL PARK

They drove down a blackly-new asphalt road, trees scowling down at them and meeting overhead. Here all traces of dawn were obliterated. Pinguel remembered the feel of branches in his hands.

'Now,' murmured Ring, 'can you direct us, Your Highness?'

Pinguel stepped across the dashboard until he was close enough to the windscreen to touch it, and made himself turn away from thoughts of a lost past. There remained the present to fight for, after all.

'We need to go into the centre. I should be able to recognise some of the trees when we get there.'

The truck ate up the distance that it had taken Pinguel, Sog and Graf over ten days to travel. Other roads, though narrower, branched off theirs. After a couple of hours, when greyish sunlight had begun to tinge the upper branches of trees, although it was still necessary to keep the truck's headlights on down below, they came to a broader crossroads with an arrow-sign that said, 'Dragon's Tooth, 5 kms'.

'Should be around here,' murmured Pinguel, holding up a hand for Orsus to slow down.

The trouble was that the strangeness of this new gap between trees, plus being at ground level, made the branches impossible to identify.

'Can we stop?' Pinguel asked. 'I need to climb, and see.'

'We pretend a flat tyre,' muttered the bear, as the truck's brakes hissed them to a halt.

'Back within an hour,' Pinguel called, as he leaned on the door handle to push it down. 'I'd better go alone. None of you are practised at climbing.'

'I am!' Ring cried, jumping after him, and as they ran to the nearest tree he elaborated: 'I lived in trees for a time, during my student days. It might surprise Your Highness to learn of some of the things I've done.'

FIFTY-FOUR ~~~

Halfway up the tree, Ring jumped recklessly for a branch, and fell. But like a trained blat, he remained calm, grabbed another and hauled himself up.

'To tell you the truth,' he puffed, only slightly out of breath, 'this is the most exciting thing I've done in weeks. You know, pretending to be luggage doesn't exactly thrill me to bits.'

'Shsh!' Pinguel whispered. 'I hear something.'

A breeze ruffled treetops.

'No, nothing.' Yet he led the way towards where he had thought the sound (fluttery and light, like a butterfly exploring a window) had come from.

He quickly recognised where he was: not far from his school. They came to a golfing platform, and Pinguel again stood still, this time shocked at the silence and, although morning light was filtering though treetops, by the gloom as well.

No bakers, no delivery blats, no cable car drivers and other early risers. Machinery should have been running, steam pipes clanking, creating a background only noticeable when it no longer existed, and windows here and there should have glowed warmly, blending light with the smell of breakfasts cooking.

This time Pinguel definitely heard the sound, Ring too.

'Reminds me of a friend of mine,' Ring whispered in a tone of voice strangely (for him) thoughtful. 'I used to carry him on my back. His legs didn't work. We became separated in a dispute with the Hendersonians, and I haven't been able to find him since. He made a sound like that, sort of a shiver, when he had to be silent but couldn't stop himself from laughing.'

They navigated by the sound, turning back when it weakened, pressing on as it increased. Past the school, they glimpsed a tiny corner of red light, and caught the barest whiff of smoke.

They crept along a branch (little more than a twig to a human). The light came from the corner of a window.

'The Bardles' golfing shop,' murmured Pinguel, remembering his first almighty hit of a golf ball.

The shuddering was too irregular to be made by a machine.

'Never stop to wonder,' advised Ring. 'Just barge right in.'

And with that, the titan — not waiting for the approval of his king — jumped from the branch to the Bardles' platform, and with a cry that managed to sound both ferocious and very small in the silent forest, leaned back and, using a fraction of his titanic strength, kicked down the door.

Inside it was dark except for a charcoal stove, the source of the red light. And around this, huddled with blankets and wings around one another, were twelve featherless parrots.

Pinguel recognised them immediately from outside the Employment Bureau. They were the ones who had sold their feathers for a lifetime's exemption from Breathing Tax.

He remembered Duke Pinchie's shimmery, many-coloured cloak, made from these feathers.

The parrots' eyes were wide with fear. Only their beaks moved, chattering from the damp chill of permanent featherlessness that no fire would ever properly dispel.

'What?' Ring couldn't help wondering. 'Lost your feathers?'

'No, no.' Pinguel placed a quietening hand on his fellow titan's shoulder. He didn't want him laughing at the birds. 'These are friends.'

The birds stared back, saying nothing, until one gave a little cough and, just as Pinguel was about to ask if they knew where Graf and the blats were, croaked:

'*Friends*?'

'Yes,' Pinguel found himself promising. 'Come with us! We have a truck, below, that's much warmer than here. We'll be able to find you clothes and food.'

'You mean it?' asked the bird — their leader — suspiciously. 'No one has ever been kind to us. We're a small flock, the last of a species. We thought we could guarantee our freedom to do as we wished by selling our feathers, but the trouble was, we had never been without feathers before. We had no idea how horrible it would be.'

'Then come with us,' Pinguel urged. 'But first, tell me, do you know of blats, an owl and a wolf, hiding out in the forest? We've come for them, you see. That's why we're here.'

The birds were stirring, tugging their blankets closer about themselves, gathering their few belongings, whispering to one another.

'My name is Niara,' the leader resumed, and when introductions were over she drew herself up. 'Several trees along, you will find whom you seek.'

Pinguel realised that having given this information, Niara and the other birds fully expected to be left behind.

'Ring, please,' Pinguel hastened, giving a shiver at the air of lucklessness in the room, 'stay and show our new friends and allies back to the truck. I'll find the others.'

The birds' gratitude hardly had time to grow before Pinguel had swung out. He thought he knew exactly where Niara had meant.

His and Cliffkin's place. He raced, forcing himself through something far more dangerous than branches slippery with ash and disuse: the gloom of a vanished past. Near the verandah he caught a warmish, sickly smell. In a corner were ropes and tackle. He jumped railings onto the floor, and without any warning found himself face to face with Ogren and the other guards, who had emerged silently from shadows, spears at the ready.

The faces of the blats were pinched with shadow, hunger and dirt, their eyes narrowed with fear that this might not really be Pinguel, but the start of a whole new danger.

'It's *me*,' the titan promised, as belief caused the blats gradually to relax and lean their spears against the railings.

Ogren went to the edge and looked about.

'Speak softly,' he whispered to Pinguel. 'The forest is full of knights with sound and heat detection equipment. We have had to flee from them many times. There was no room for the hawks; they flew far, far off with their wounded comrade, Harth, to escape the jets. Last time ... Come inside, yes. Last time, as you can see, Graf was wounded.'

The wolf lay in the corner where Cliffkin's bed had once been. To fit him inside, the blats had removed not only the door, but the frame around it too, and even then it must have been a tight squeeze. The living wood of the tree was tinged with green where it had recently been bared.

Graf was asleep, one front leg bandaged.

A blat stood near him, and rubbed the wolf's back as a fluttering came from behind, causing only Pinguel to start.

It was Sog.

'Pinguel!' the owl affectionately brushed the boy's shoulder with a wing. 'I have been telling everyone that you would come.' He noticed the blue cloak. 'You used the Ant Bell? Tell me' — and here the owl widened his eyes just a fraction to show his pleasure — '*Your Highness*, where do we go now? Yes, yes, I knew who you were, but imagine if word had got out to Pinchie, before we were ready. As it was, we were recognised as soon as we got to Vizzencourt. I underestimated, most gravely, the number of spies. Tell me, is Peregrine with you? Where is he?' The owl blinked at the shadows behind Pinguel.

'No, Peregrine isn't here, Sog.'

The owl ruffled his feathers, but settled them quickly back again. His eyes caught the light of the coals.

'Well, that makes things more difficult, I suppose. Still, we have ropes and pulleys to lower Graf.' His voice dropped to a whisper. 'The wound is infected. Perhaps we could get Tinderwell, the dragon, to fly him straight to the ship?'

'Tinderwell didn't come,' murmured the titan, going over to his wolf friend and patting his back. Graf's chest rose and fell with each rapid breath. Black in this light, his fur was matted hard with dried blood around the bandage.

'So Tinderwell didn't come, nor Peregrine?' wondered the owl. 'Who *did* come, may I ask?'

'Ring, and Genius, and lots of others. We have a truck near the Bardles' place. How far away is the nearest road?'

'Half a mile, that w-way,' Ogren stuttered.

Pinguel sensed the weakness and desperation of the blats around him.

So he stood up straight, and forced himself to smile.

'Things couldn't be better,' he proclaimed, feeling just the opposite. 'And back at the boat there is, I hear, a dining room capable of holding five hundred for a victory feast! Lower Graf to the base of the tree, and wait there. I have to dig up something from the basement, then I'll bring help.'

While the blats and Sog, weak from hunger, fetched the ropes, Pinguel rushed to the linen cupboard and the trapdoor that led to the cellar. Too late he realised that he should have brought a light with him, but he left the trapdoor open and this provided just enough for him to see the rungs of the ladder until he was halfway down, and after that his eyes were acute enough to make out the earthy floor in the dim glow from above.

He felt with his fingers for signs of recent digging, and when he came to softer earth he pushed his hands in until he touched a canvas strap, which he tugged up. It was a knapsack far too heavy for a blat to lift, but light for a titan. Cliffkin must have carried the boxes containing Faringaria and the others down separately, pushed them into the bag, and buried them.

When Pinguel reached the top again, the blats were lowering Graf in a rope harness, with Sog hovering just above to give instructions. When he reached the ground, the wolf half-opened one eye, and, wincing at the pain from his wound, muttered to Pinguel: 'Good to see you, finally.'

Pinguel knelt. 'We'll have you warm and cared for in a few minutes. Mind this knapsack, please. It's extremely precious.'

Keeping to the shadows, he found the truck, jumped to the dashboard, and directed Orsus to where the blats and Graf were waiting.

'The parrots,' he suddenly remembered. 'Did they . . .?'

'They're in the back, with Ring,' Genius answered. He was lying on the seat, giving his neck a rest.

Leaning together over the road, as though to comfort one another, the trees made it like night at ground level. The truck's brakes hissed when the headlights caught the forlorn group of blats, wounded wolf, owl and knapsack by the road.

Pinguel jumped out and banged on the back doors.

'Open up! I need help.'

A human called out:

'Step back, and we'll open the doors.'

Ring jumped out first (he had been getting the featherless parrots some food), followed by bears, wolves and humans, and within seconds the blats and Graf were inside. The blats stepped back at first, overcome by fear in particular of the wolves. But seeing Pinguel with them, and giving orders, with all obeying, they managed to fight off their urge to melt into the shadows.

'I'm going to stay in here,' Pinguel told Ring. 'Get Orsus to head for Vizzencourt. We need to find a work camp —'

'I know the one you mean,' spoke up Sog. 'On the outskirts of the forest, Vizzencourt side. I flew past it on my way here.'

'Good. You direct Orsus, and ask him to stop as soon as the camp comes into sight.' Pinguel was already climbing into the back of the truck.

'Heading straight for the work camp?' Ring wondered, hardly able to believe his luck. Nose ring trembling, he shook a fist. 'There'll be knights all around, on guard.'

'Yes,' the boy-king answered vaguely, 'I suppose so.' With one hand he was already rummaging in the knapsack, with the other taking from his jacket pocket the bottle of syrup that the human had given him, back at the coast.

Ring jumped from the cab, and ran to tell Orsus the marvellous news.

FIFTY-FIVE ～～～

'Is it true?' Niara whispered to Pinguel as the titan pulled at the straps of the knapsack, surrounded by creatures (with two humans holding a lantern each) watching curiously. 'Is it true, as the little fellow with the nose-ring told us, that there is a ship on the ocean, captained by a boy called Hugo the Dancer, and that on this ship there are tailors clever enough to make us new suits of feathers?'

'Yes,' Pinguel promised, although he didn't know for sure. But if Ring had said so, well, there was at least a good chance that it was true.

He took a box from a knapsack pocket and placed it carefully beside him. He remembered this one. Dark wood, with a brass latch, it contained a troupe of acrobats. He suddenly felt almost too frightened to reach again into the knapsack. What if the box containing Faringaria wasn't inside? Or if it was, and he opened it only to find that, buried so long in the cold earth . . .

He shook his head, took the bottle of syrup from his jacket pocket, and handed it to Niara.

'Can you mind this, please? It's very precious.'

The parrot, only a little shorter than Pinguel, straightened a grey blanket around her shoulders, and nodded. The truck began to move and everyone, even the practised stowaways, staggered a little. One of the birds lost his footing entirely, and rolled until caught and set on his feet by a wolf. Pinguel kept taking boxes from the canvas knapsack until, last of all (which meant that Cliffkin must have put them in first) he came to Faringaria and the chess box.

In the far corner of the cab a wolf who knew something about medicine had placed a lantern beside Graf and was changing the dressing on his wound. Pinguel turned to the creatures around him.

'Move back, please. I'll need as much air as possible. Except for you, Niara. Someone please bring a lantern closer?'

The truck raced through what had once been Deep Forest but was now mere segments between asphalted highways. Other trucks honked greetings to the one containing stowaways, and Orsus touched his own horn in reply.

Pinguel was opening the lid to Faringaria's box. Despite the noise of the truck's motor, and of the wheels' flicking up occasional pebbles onto the underside, the interior was hushed as the lid opened and the lamplight showed a tiny cupboard, then the foot of a bed, then finally the form of a woman no more than an inch tall, golden hair across the pillow, asleep in bed.

Pinguel dipped his fingertip into the syrup. Light fell across Faringaria's face. He opened the box and waited.

In what he thought of now as the Old Days, Faringaria had woken up with the light. Cliffkin would place a drop of syrup on her lips and she would lick it off, regain her strength, and sit up ready for conversation and a game of chess.

Now she just lay there, face pale as the pillow.

Pinguel touched her cheek and thought of how she had once been a human, climbing, mud-covered, from the river Docker. Her skin felt cold, and a chilly sense of disaster made the boy shiver.

He turned to Niara, and his voice was even hoarser than normal:

'Could you please touch her face, and see if she really is as cold as she feels to me?'

With the pink tip of a featherless wing, Niara touched Faringaria's cheek. Then she moved the tip down a little, to rest a moment on her neck.

'Yes. Cold. The heart is beating, though faintly. I can feel a vein in the neck.'

And now Pinguel felt strongly the agony that comes from not knowing what to do, while also being the one who has to act. He could close the box and wait for Cliffkin — if they managed to free Cliffkin — but his whole reason for wanting to open the box was that he needed Faringaria's advice and the help of herself and her followers in the raid on the work camp. These tiny creatures would be able to slip inside, steal keys, discover weak points and, most importantly, contact Cliffkin. Finally, Pinguel decided that yes, he should lower the lid and wait for the liberation of his father.

The truck sped from the forest, passing not far from where the travellers had sheltered on the night that Sog told the story of Peregrine and the little grey stone. On the misty horizon stood a new structure made of huts of the type that are carried, already built, on the backs of semi-trailers. They were surrounded by high fences fringed with barbed wire, and illuminated by arc lights attached to watch-towers that stood at each corner. The land around the work camp was brown and misty, and the soil showed the imprints of tractor tyres and bulldozer treads. Following Sog's instructions, Orsus turned onto a side road and headed slowly for the camp.

As Pinguel went to close the lid of Faringaria's box, the tiny woman stirred in her bed, and raised a hand against the return of the darkness that she had endured for so long.

'Faringaria!'

Pinguel pushed the lid right back, and brought his finger with the drop of syrup on its tip close to her mouth. But instead of licking it, as she had always done with Cliffkin, she arched her back and groaned.

Pinguel found himself looking over his shoulder, hoping, despite knowing it was impossible, that he would see Cliffkin there, with a solution. Instead he saw Niara, and beyond her the other birds, humans, wolves and bears, all looking at him as though expecting an order, an instruction, a 'Bring this' or a 'Do that'.

He brought his face very close to Faringaria and whispered:

'Please, what should I do? How can I help you?'

He didn't feel like a king. He felt as he had on that Magic Night, years ago: a boy who has fallen into seriousness and is desperate for a way out.

The truck halted with the work camp only about two hundred yards away, mist drifting through the wire fence and around the drab huts.

'I'll get the king,' announced Ring, climbing to the dashboard and rubbing his hands with excitement at the thought of the fight he sensed was imminent.

'Perhaps you should wait until . . .' began Genius, still rugged up in his red blanket.

'Uh oh . . .' Sog had unwound a window, and was perched on the bar that held a side mirror.

A whirring noise was growing steadily louder. Mist rushed away, as though frightened. Orsus looked up. He thought he knew what the cause was, and if he was right, why, they were in . . .

'Serious trouble,' murmured Genius, who even with his head muffled in blankets had been able to identify the sound from the frequency of the dull beats that it contained.

A cone of white light engulfed the truck, followed by a second and third. A voice boomed out:

'Do not attempt to move! We have you in the sight of our rockets. In the name of Grand Duke Pinchie du Henderson, come out of the truck, everyone, with your hands in the air.'

As Genius whispered 'helicopters', Sog raised a wing to shield his eyes. From the direction of the work camp, a whole army of Knights of Work came galloping towards them.

'So they guessed we would come,' smiled Ring. 'Well, *now* there'll be a fight.'

Orsus put his paws on the steering wheel, and looked at Genius, who only waved one hand, and nodded back at the cab in a gesture that meant:

'Don't do anything. We must wait for instructions from our king.'

FIFTY-SIX ～～

Just as Pinguel heard the approach of the helicopters, Faringaria turned to him and whispered something, tendons standing out in her neck, face thin with pain.

He couldn't hear it.

'Not...' she seemed to say, at the same time pointing with one hand at the floor of her box.

'I can't hear!' he said.

'Not ... Nit ...'

'Nit ...?' Pinguel wondered as something huge and heavy struck the truck, and a commanding voice boomed:

'Open up or we'll smash our way in!'

The helicopters had swooped away; now the truck was surrounded by over a hundred Knights of Work, steam hissing from joints and puffing from the nostrils of warhorses into the startled air.

Ring, Genius and Sog hid beneath the dashboard. Orsus sat with his hands up to show that he wasn't holding any weapons. He had lost his casually-gruff look, and his usually pointed ears were pressed right back from fear. Is this my first day of life slavery in a work camp? he was wondering.

As Faringaria spoke again, her words were drowned by the hammering of knights from outside. But this time, making a huge effort, she had summoned up the strength to prop herself on one elbow and point. She pointed downwards, to her bed, and curled her hand over to point *underneath*.

'What . . .?' Pinguel had begun to ask, when the answer came to him.

Faringaria collapsed back, and as her golden hair spread across her face Pinguel saw that it had already lost its lustre. He turned to Naria:

'Can you pick her up and hold her very gently?'

The mood inside the truck was solemn and sad.

Our king has failed, it said. Not just impulsive, but crazy, to rush straight up to a work camp like this. And we were mad to have entrusted such a young creature — even a titan — with the kingship.

Despite all the pain of being lowered by ropes, and of being moved this way and that to have new bandages wrapped around him, Graf was sitting up watching his friend. Of all the creatures in the truck, he was the one who best knew Pinguel, and he was the only one whose eyes flickered with genuine hope of victory.

Naria held the princess gently in her wings as Pinguel picked up the bed and pulled from beneath it two blat-sized knitting needles and a skein of wool that glowed richly — in deep greens, reds and blues — in the lamplight.

Everyone was watching him. He thought, but was careful not to say aloud:

'I don't know how to knit.'

Yet wasn't knitting just tangling up wool, and using needles to do it? After all, the old sorcerer, Fomsaxtil, hadn't finished up with a scarf or a pair of socks, had he?

And now for the first time since his failure to cross Cold Mountains, Pinguel felt some of his old, confident impulsiveness. And he *had* crossed the mountains, hadn't he, in the end? He had needed help to do so, but what was wrong with that? He would need help now, too.

He started to call out, but was interrupted by a smashing against the back of the truck, and shouted threats from the Knights of Work to open up immediately or else.

'Take all the boxes out of the rucksack and open them. Quick!' Pinguel shouted. And when he noticed everyone's doubtful looks, and how close they were to being paralysed with fear, he found himself giving a proud laugh, and yelling louder:

'Do you think that I didn't *foresee* this? We have never been safer than at this moment, but only if you do as I say. Take the boxes from the rucksack and open them, and do it gently but *quickly.*'

Paws, hands and wings had the boxes. When they withdrew, the lids were raised.

Now a battering ram smashed against the doors of the truck, causing one bar of the lock to shatter. The blow created a gap wide enough for a lance to plunge inside, spearing wildly towards a group of bears. One caught it and, with a roar of anger, pulled it all the way through. In the silence that followed, everyone knew that the battering ram was being taken back, and that this next blow would burst open the truck doors.

Yet no one thought of turning into luggage. The bears would never leave behind Orsus, in the cab, nor would the wolves desert Graf. Nor would any creature wish to abandon the featherless birds to the Knights of Work. However badly things might turn out, even if it meant the end of the Order of Stowaways, they would endure it together.

And not *might turn out badly* but *certainly will*, went the mood in the cabin when the creatures saw what Pinguel was doing.

For Pinguel had taken up the brightly coloured wool and, using two needles made of gleaming silver, had begun — as inexpertly as anyone could possibly do it — to knit.

When a huge tree begins to fall, chopped by axes almost through its trunk, a deep groan of hopelessness sweeps through a forest. That was the sound that filled the back of the truck, when Pinguel began to knit.

'Move away from the doors!' the king commanded, but everyone had already done this, for fear of the next blow from the battering ram.

The Knights of Work were ominously silent. There was no longer any need for them to shout. Everything was under control. Any second the doors would burst open and they would have the pleasure of dragging out whoever happened to be inside.

FIFTY-SEVEN ~~~

A silence also filled the work camp itself. Usually at this time those creatures whose turn it was would be banging wooden spoons against metal plates to summon everyone to the usual breakfast of watery gruel made from wheat grain that had been left to soak overnight. Blats and wolves, from their large and small barracks, would form silent queues under the hostile gaze of knights who — mostly on account of dishonesty or laziness — had been sentenced to a period of guard duty at the camp.

But this morning the place was silent. Those whose job it was to prepare breakfast found the barrack doors locked.

'Something's up,' whispered Cliffkin, from a top bunk, to Clerkwellstone down below.

The sorcerer blat was thinner than he had ever been. The bones and tendons on the backs of his hands stood out as he gripped the bunk's railing.

'I've been listening,' Clerkwellstone confirmed. 'The cans have gone.' (This was camp slang for the knights.)

As blats began to make for the windows (the wolves were doing the same in the other, larger barracks) Clerkwellstone hummed to himself, 'Cause and effect, effect and cause...' and for some reason found himself remembering the day, not so long ago, when Pinguel had fallen in a shower of twigs onto his platform.

FIFTY-EIGHT ~~~

As the battering ram was about to fling back the truck doors, Pinguel closed his eyes and thought of Fomsaxtil's toys.

For wasn't that what the old sorcerer, in Cliffkin's story, had focused on when casting his spell? But the trouble with this was that Pinguel had no idea what

Fomsaxtil's toys had been like, whether they had been puzzles, or clubs and balls, model cable cars, or members of the Spear or Arrow Guard carved from wood. So he found himself instead thinking of his and his father's house: of the lumps of amber containing insects on the shelves, of the slice of strawberry shortbread and cup of tea that he and Cliffkin often had for supper, of Madam's dining room with its delicious smells from the kitchen, of the complicated and mysterious gadgets on the shelves in Clerkwellstone's house, and of the yellowing strands of ancient wool caught in splinters at the warrior training platform where Boboscular had lectured.

And as Pinguel thought of these things, and kept his eyes closed and imagined himself back at home, he found that the wool was looping over the forefinger of his right hand, and sliding over the knitting needle, and that the kneedle in his left hand was tucking this strand of wool down, to form a sort of knot and the start of what, even to the eyes of an expert, looked like highly accomplished knitting.

This was all, for now, that Pinguel knew. In a time of great danger, the greatest he had ever been in, he discovered that he was naturally good at knitting.

But the other occupants of the truck saw far more than this.

They saw the wool flare like strands of light, coiling around King Opthalomicus like strongly protective arms. They saw this magic wool, or light, swirl over everyone, felt it brush their heads and touch their shoulders and somehow they were all, straightaway, reassured. Whatever happened, however disastrously things turned out, it would somehow all be for the best because at least they had seen and felt this magic.

The coloured lights next reared up in a tangle over Pinguel, as though absorbing, or at least taking a hint from, his thoughts, then swooped in a rush over the opened boxes spread out around the old rucksack that had been buried for so long in the cold earth. The light separated into strands, merged again, then rushed at the tiny, hibernating figures, and the moment they touched them, including Faringaria in the arms of a startled Naria, they slowed down time as well.

The battering ram crashed into the truck's back doors, but this happened so slowly that the doors merely drifted gracefully inwards. The strands of wool broadened, and intensified their colours, and now the creatures in the back of the truck had to shade their eyes against the brilliance of the light around each strand. Faces appeared, distorted as though painted on air.

One thing was certain: Niara soon found that the tiny woman in her wings was far from tiny. Not that she was the size of a giant-like bear or human — no. But she was fully as tall, all of a sudden, as Pinguel or as Niara herself. And as the bird lowered her gently to the floor, the young woman opened her eyes, saw the featherless bird, and smiled.

'Hello,' she had time to say, as the battering ram broke the last remaining bolt, and the doors collapsed inside.

As the ribbons of colour shrank back into wool-sized dimensions, and returned to the knitting needles in Pinguel's hands, Graf noticed, standing before him, a human in multi-coloured acrobat's tights, right next to a knight in armour who, with his sword held with the hilt close to his cheek, was adjusting a join at the side of his visor.

The whole inside of the truck was suddenly, extremely, bulgingly, crowded with humans whom no one (except for Pinguel) could remember having seen before. There were eleven archers with longbows gathered near the doors, each pulling an arrow with a golden thread attached to its fletch, and these were jostled by a party of lightly armoured foot soldiers carrying nets made of a silvery material, who were in turn being nudged in the back by armoured knights, each with a huge, curled-up whip in his right hand ... and then of course there were acrobats, with their brightly coloured pins and balls for juggling, and even larger balls for balancing on, followed by a knot of smaller humans in the dark brown robes and cowls of what looked like an order of monks, and, over in the corner opposite Graf, a party of humans in white robes who, perhaps more than anyone in the truck, looked bewildered to find themselves where they were.

The faces of the humans were too varied to describe. Some had harshly irregular features, a missing eye here, gaps in teeth there, with scars scoring this way and that like the lines on a weather map; others were the opposite, looking as if they had been drawn by the illustrator of a storybook in which everyone is tall and handsome and noble-looking. But all of them were gripped by the same purpose, and had the same goal, for as the battering ram shoved the doors further inwards, the pressure of the new arrivals inside the truck immediately shoved the doors — to the great surprise of the assembled Knights of Work — back out again.

And as the warhorses of the knights stumbled with astonishment, and their riders struggled to bring them under control, the archers fired arrows between the figures, aiming for gaps between knights and horses, and just when it looked like the arrows might shoot harmlessly into the distance, trailing their golden lengths of cord, they curled around and around, entangling the legs of the horses and the weapon-laden arms of the knights themselves.

Next came the lightly-armed soldiers with the nets, who, undisturbed by the enraged shouts of the knights, or by the fierce snorting of the warhorses, jumped onto armoured shoulders and heads and from there straight to the roof of the truck. They rushed to the front where, after a moment's hesitation, during which they grinned at one another in anticipation of the pleasure to come, they cast their nets over the knights around the cab, and then, by an expert pulling of side cords, tightened these into efficient bundles like those collections of apples or oranges that sell for especially low prices at the supermarket.

'Wonderful! Wonderful!' cried Ring, jumping from the cabin to the shoulder of a knight who, for all his shouting and writhing, could not get his arm far enough away from his body to swing his sword and cut the net.

Genius closed his eyes, pulled the blanket snugger around his shoulders, and gave a little smile.

Already, wolves were tearing between the unsteady legs of the horses, then, gaining speed as they reached clear ground, they headed for the work camp to liberate their fellows. One of the humans in long robes (all of whom were still looking bewildered) had been a doctor in an earlier stage of his life. He went straight over to see what he could do for Graf.

What afterwards came to be known as 'The Battle of the Knitting Needles' was nearly — but not quite — over, and the two creatures who had had most to do with it at the start, and least in the middle, found themselves standing together as the truck roared away from a tangle of netted and tied up Knights of Work.

'I thought ... I wouldn't be able to revive you,' stammered Pinguel. He had only just opened his eyes and recovered from the surprise of seeing what his knitting had created.

He found that he had his arm around Faringaria's shoulder, and that her face was quite close to his.

'Look,' she said. 'The wolves have opened the gates of the camp. The blats will be here soon, including Cliffkin.'

FIFTY-NINE ~~~

Orsus had to slow the truck down because, coming towards them from the camp, the wire fence trampled down by the force of their onrush, was a storm of wolves.

With his sharp titan's eyes, Ring was the first to see what was strange about these creatures.

'They have riders,' laughed Ring. 'Look, Orsus! Look, Genius! There are blats on the backs of those wolves!'

Genius muttered, although only Ring heard him over the noise of the truck's motor:

'As it was, many centuries ago. Blats were wolf riders. Remember the Battle of the Hot Plains, when the Hendersonians were outflanked, and their cavalry put to rout by such riders?'

Genius's green, titan's eyes softened into a look of ageless remembering. The things he had seen! He found himself recalling a boy called Jason, who (before his first meeting with titans) had been so subject to gloom that he had been unable to rise from his bed. Later, he had become a true hero. And then there were people and blats, and rooms and places each with a living atmosphere, and there were titans appearing from his memory like objects from a mist ... each with its place in a drama that, he sensed, would soon come to a turning point, a crucial stage.

He sat up suddenly.

'What is it?' demanded Ring.

Never had he seen Genius look so frightened.

As the wolves with blats on their backs neared the truck, and Pinguel and Faringaria and the humans and bears helped them aboard, Genius whispered to his old friend:

'A time of great trouble ...'

'You mean,' Ring asked, 'battles, fights? It'll look as though we're going to lose at first, but we'll win in the end?'

Genius only shook his head and, in the midst of the arrival of the blats, and as the truck began to roar away, making for the coast, fell fast asleep. And even Ring, with his limitless optimism and keenness for action, with his belief that in the long run the forces of the rule-breakers, of the lovers of mayhem, would win through, felt a chill over the back of his neck and down his spine. To dispel it, he jumped from the window, grabbed hold of a bar that supported the mirror, swung to the roof of the cab, slipped and nearly tumbled off the truck, sprinted through the chilly air to the back, balanced on a door that was hanging by only a third of a hinge, and jumped inside.

'Whew!' he cried as he flew through the air, landing on a bear's head and having to grab onto an ear to steady himself, then hopping quickly off via a human's shoulder and a wolf's back before the bear could swat him. 'Isn't it crowded in here?'

Blats had gathered in the corner where Graf lay being tended by the human doctor, and here Cliffkin was embracing his son, and Pinguel his father. The truck jolted and swayed, sending them staggering now one way, now the other. For a long moment they were silent, and during this time the noises of creatures and machinery, for them, faded to nothing.

'It was Blat Magic...' Pinguel finally said, taking his father's hand. 'It was Blat Magic that saved us.'

Madam, thinner and greyer, had come up to them.

'Look at you, Pinguel! You're taller. And how strong you look. Why, you've almost grown up.'

'And you, my dear,' murmured Clerkwellstone, tenderly putting a hand on Pinguel's shoulder, but addressing Faringaria, beside him. 'I don't think that we have been introduced.'

It was Cliffkin who spoke. 'This is Faringaria, a princess.'

But at that moment Strolgo came up, eyes heavy with worry for his son, when whom should he see, face half-covered by shadow and pressed forward towards him, but Ogren himself. As everyone started to talk — no, to shout their happiness — Ring cried out:

'Shsh! Listen!'

A familiar thuddering of the air, then a huge face with gentle brown eyes and delicate tendrils of smoke drifting from its nostrils, appeared at the back of the truck.

'Good morning. My name is Tinderwell, for those of you who don't know me, and remains Tinderwell for those of you who do. I've brought the chains, so if you'll stop for a moment, we'll fasten them and I'll carry you over the Cold Mountains to the *Orestea*, Hugo's ocean liner. We'll have to hurry, though, because jets will be along soon.'

SIXTY ~~~

Carried by Tinderwell, the truck swayed over the peaks of the Cold Mountains. Because of the broken back doors it was much colder inside than before, and everyone had to huddle together. Pinguel found himself sharing his blue ant robe with Faringaria. A thin, grey-haired blat with a pointy nose appeared before him.

'Our blat tactics worked for a while,' he murmured. 'But we had never thought that anyone would take possession of the *whole* forest. It was the forest, you see, that always stood at the centre of our strategy: melting into it, using its shadows, retreating through it.'

It was Boboscular, the retired captain-turned-teacher. He sighed as he watched Deep Forest slip into the distance.

'How big *is* the world?' Pinguel found himself wondering to himself, aloud.

It was Faringaria who answered, whispering into his ear:

'Big enough for anything, Pinguel. Huge, with shadows and unexplored places, and whole countries that have never known the distinction of being placed upon a map.'

'And it's to those places,' chimed in Ring, appearing before his king with a respectful look that was quite strange for him, 'that we'll be going now, with Hugo.'

For a few seconds, the creatures in the back of the truck nearly froze, and icicles appeared on Tinderwell's toes and the tip of his tail. But then they descended, and so rapidly that their ears popped and several blats and wolves, who weren't used to this sort of thing, felt quite sick. Tinderwell carried them low over the foothills, then lower still over the short plain and ocean.

Blats and wolves stared, amazed. How could such a huge mass of water exist? It was so deep that each wave moved with elephantine slowness, as though heavily aware of what a responsibility it is to be a wave in such a mass of water. The sky was grey and the ocean itself deep green.

'Must be a thousand miles deep,' Clerkwellstone sighed.

But the biggest surprise was yet to come. Tinderwell circled, and a great sigh went up from the occupants of the truck as they saw the *Orestea* (an ocean liner built in the days when ocean liners were truly huge) floating, white and proud, on the ocean.

'Why,' marvelled Clerkwellstone, 'it seems to be ignoring the waves. It hardly rocks at all.'

From the back of the truck, Graf caught sight of it between the legs of other creatures, and said to Pinguel and Faringaria, who had joined him:

226

'It's what I used to dream of, remember? Look at those windows. Must be a million rooms. A huge place, where everyone can be together.'

And then he closed his eyes, exhausted by all the excitement.

'He'll be fine,' the human doctor whispered to Pinguel. 'Just needs rest, and something to eat.'

'And to paint some paintings,' Pinguel added to himself.

Slowly, slowly, Tinderwell lowered the truck to the huge stern deck of the liner, so carefully that when it landed no one was aware that it had done so until Ring, who had rushed right to the truck-edge, called out:

'What are you waiting for? Can't you smell the food?'

SIXTY-ONE ~~~

As the *Orestea* sailed at top speed for the open sea, and the coast became a blur on the horizon, then the thinnest possible line, and finally disappeared, the creatures from the truck who had never been on a boat before found themselves dazed not only with relief at their escape, and happiness at finding themselves among friends, but also at the strangeness of their new home.

The blats were most astonished at the presence of other blats on board. These came from the forest on the other side of Cold Mountains and (the Deep Forest blats discovered over a feast that started off as lunch, continued as dinner, and still hadn't finished when it came time for supper) had escaped, helped by Hugo the Dancer, just before the fire had destroyed their forest.

'So it *was* a fire!' exclaimed Clerkwellstone to a new friend, a blat called Romfi, a scientist himself. 'You know, it melted some of the ice of Cold Mountains, and nearly flooded our forest.'

'Where is Hugo?' Ogren wondered to his beaming father, seated between him and Sarin in the huge dining hall. He was anxious to meet the world champion golfer.

'Look, over there! His *doll*!' laughed Strolgo, who hadn't been able to stop laughing since finding his son safe and well.

Two tables away, carrying a human-sized bowl of sugar cubes, and with his metal helmet tipped right back on his head, was the member of the Spear Guard who had given Hugo advice on the golf course.

Pinguel was leaning across to speak to Sog, who was talking with Niara and some of the other featherless birds, when he felt a tap on his shoulder.

It was Ouk. Greeny-yellow eyes sparkling in his blue face, the ex-stone whispered:

'It's Hugo. He begs the honour of your company.'

So Ouk led Pinguel down dim corridors, and up stairs and down stairs, and finally knocked at a metal door that, to him and Pinguel, was several storeys high.

The door was opened by a human girl about twelve years old, who had red, curly hair, and whose face looked about to break into laughter, although there was worry there too, especially around her eyes.

'Please come in,' came another voice, that of a boy.

It was Hugo, rising from an armchair beside a window that overlooked the ocean.

'King Opthalomicus,' said the boy. 'Greetings.'

Seen in a photograph, or glimpsed across a room, with no chance to sense his character, Hugo would have looked remarkably ugly. His back was hunched over and one eye drooped, twisting his face askew. He moved with a half-sideways, shuffling gait. But Pinguel hardly noticed this. Hugo was holding something red and deeply glinting in one hand. He squeezed his fingers around it as he spoke again.

'This is Nadia, my friend.'

Nadia nodded. 'Happy to meet you, Your Highness.' And just when it seemed that she might burst into laughter, she pointed to a chair.

'Please, sit down.'

'Not here!' came a little voice from what had looked like a pile of red blankets.

It was Genius. He sat up straighter, and ran his hands through his hair.

'King Opthalomicus...' Hugo began again, when Pinguel had positioned himself beside Genius.

'Please, call me Pinguel.'

Hugo nodded. 'Pinguel, I want to welcome you to the *Orestea*, and to congratulate you on your brilliance in rescuing the blats of Deep Forest and their wolf allies.'

Before Pinguel could protest that this hadn't exactly been all his work, Hugo went on:

'We have enough petrol to sail to the ends of the world. And that is exactly, if you are in agreement, where we will be going. Pinchie du Henderson your uncle and his many allies, will be searching for us. A darkness is creeping over the world, a cold shadow like that from an eclipse of the sun. It will be a long time before it will be safe for us to put into a port. Today's feast of celebration will be our last for a long time. From tomorrow, food and water will be rationed. I would like you to accept the command of this vessel, Pinguel.'

Just as the titan began to hesitate, he caught Genius's eye, beside him.

'You must accept,' whispered the titan.

So Pinguel nodded. 'Thank you.'

Hugo went to the window and looked down at the red, glinting thing in his hand. It was a marble, a simple marble made of glass. Nadia went to him, put a hand on the boy's shoulder, and spoke to Pinguel:

'There is someone else whose help we need. We have been waiting for him for a long time.'

'We cannot,' put in Genius, 'act against the Hendersonians and their allies without him.'

'Peregrine the Wizard.' Hugo had turned from the window. He smiled, and with a slight movement of his fingers, hardly perceptible, brought a kind of cheerfulness into the cabin, an expectation of adventure, of cosiness, of stories told late at night among friends.

This human boy has greatness in him, Pinguel told himself. Part of it was force of personality, a capacity for changing the moods of others, but there was also a highly strange, lonely sort of bravery, and . . .

Hugo continued:

'Peregrine is in trouble, we suspect in the Pelasgian Islands. It will take us weeks to get there. Not only does he need us, but we need him, badly.' He glanced at Genius, who nodded confirmation.

'But for now,' the boy went on, once again dispelling the solemn mood, 'let us celebrate. Would you like to see my marble? I have kept it from the days before I met Nadia and blats, when I had no friends and believed the world to be a stale old place. During my worst times, this marble, with its depths of light and shadow, consoled me.'